TRIBAL
COURT

David Brunelle Legal Thriller #2

STEPHEN PENNER

ISBN-13: 978-0615758350
ISBN-10: 0615758355

Tribal Court

Joy Lorton, Editor.
Cover by Nathan Wampler Book Covers.

TRIBAL
COURT

It is a defense to a charge of murder that the homicide was justifiable.

The State has the burden of proving beyond a reasonable doubt that the homicide was not justifiable. If you find that the State has not proved the absence of this defense beyond a reasonable doubt, it will be your duty to return a verdict of not guilty.

State of Washington
Pattern Criminal Jury Instruction 16.01

CHAPTER 1

"Don't you hate it when the victim kinda deserved it?"

Seattle Police detective Larry Chen crossed his thick arms under his police-issue raincoat and looked to his friend for a reply. Dave Brunelle, King County homicide prosecutor, didn't look up from the dead body splayed at their feet. Instead he nodded and pushed his hands deeper into his own raincoat—thrown on at one in the morning when he got Chen's call.

"Just try not to say that on the stand," he said.

The murder victim was a man, late forties, overweight, and most definitely dead. His blood glistened black in the cracks between the cobblestones of Founder's Park in Seattle's Pioneer Square district. He was on his back, arms sprawled, shirt cut away by the same paramedics who left behind the adhesive chest pads they'd used to attempt resuscitation despite the multiple stab wounds to his chest. The rain was coating his face in droplets that trickled into his ear and the folds of his neck. He lay at the base of the plaza's 56-foot totem pole, like an offering to the spirits represented in the carvings, their faces made all the more grotesque by the forensic team's floodlights and the red and blue strobe of the cop cars clogging the narrow streets surrounding the square.

"So why did he deserve it?" Brunelle asked, more concerned with the potential jury nullification issues than the justness of the man's death. "Was it self defense?"

"No," Chen was quick to answer. "Witnesses said there was an argument, but nothing physical until the killer pulled out the knife and stuck it into our guy's chest."

Chen extracted his notebook from his damp pocket. "It's not what he did. It's who he was."

Brunelle finally looked up from the corpse. "Who was he?"

"George Traver," Chen read from the latest page of his running notebook. "Child molester. Registered sex offender. Failed to update his registration six months ago. Last known address was a trailer down near Tacoma. Had a warrant out for that, plus two more for shoplifting and drunk in public."

"Ah," replied Brunelle, wiping some rain from his nose. "Still, not exactly worthy of a knife in the chest."

"He was the suspect in two more child luring and indecent exposure cases."

"Okay," Brunelle agreed. "That might do it. Kind of a community service killing, huh?"

"Exactly," Chen confirmed.

Brunelle peered around the plaza. It was almost closing time. Intoxicated gawkers stumbled past the crime scene tape trying to get a glimpse of what lay at the base of the totem pole. "So where was he living?"

"He was homeless," Chen answered. "Sleeping on benches downtown mostly."

"Probably why he didn't register," Brunelle observed.

"Probably," Chen agreed, "although they're allowed to register as 'homeless.'"

Brunelle frowned. "I always thought that was stupid. It kind of defeats the purpose"

"Sure does."

"So, who's our suspect?" Brunelle asked. He needed a suspect before he could get involved. Unsolved would mean no defendant to charge. "Another homeless guy?"

"Nope, the homeless guys liked him," Chen answered. "I sent two patrol guys to interview some of them. Most scattered, but the few who stayed said ol' George here was a great guy. Salt of the earth."

"I'm sure," Brunelle scoffed. "What's the suspect description?"

Chen looked down at his notepad. "Male, twenty-something, Hispanic or Native."

"Wow, not very helpful," Brunelle observed. "That describes about twenty-five percent of the people in Pioneer Square tonight."

"Maybe," Chen shrugged, "if you include Hispanics. But if you limit it to Natives, then it's probably one, maybe two percent."

It was Brunelle's turn to shrug. "And if we reduce it to Native men with one testicle and a prosthetic elbow, we can really start to narrow it down."

Chen cocked his head at his friend. "One testicle?"

Brunelle threw up his hands. "I'm just saying, you can always narrow it down. Why would you limit the description just to Natives if the witnesses said Native or Hispanic?"

Chen looked down at the lifeless body before them. "Our victim is Native."

Brunelle pursed his lips. "I don't see why that matters. It's not like murder stays in one race. If somebody killed you, I wouldn't assume the murderer was Chinese."

Chen smirked. "You should. If I wind up murdered, you can be pretty sure it was my wife."

"Oh yeah?" Brunelle laughed.

"Yeah," Chen laughed too, but it faded and he shoved his hands in his pockets. He pushed a foot out toward the dead man splayed out at the base of the totem pole. "You gotta know someone to hate them enough to kill them."

A set of fingernails dug into Brunelle's back. "Hey there, Mr. Brunelle," came a sweet female voice from behind him. Assistant Medical Examiner Kat Anderson had arrived. She pulled her nails down the length of Brunelle's back as she walked past him. "Long time, no call."

Brunelle stiffened at the voice, then relaxed slightly as she passed him and knelt next to the corpse. He knew she was right. "Yeah," he offered. "Sorry about that. Been busy."

She turned and smiled at him. Her smile held warmth, but other thoughts too. "Of course you have. Me too."

She returned to her examination of the murder victim. She wore a long raincoat that covered her curves, but the hood was pushed back, leaving her black hair and soft face exposed to the rain. He supposed her knees were getting wet and cold from the rain-drenched cobblestones. He remembered the last time they'd really talked and he regretted not having called her since then. Their last case together had ended badly. Or at least, it had almost ended badly, and he'd been reluctant to draw Kat, or her daughter, into danger again. He knew he'd been distant for the right reasons; he just didn't know if she knew it.

"A-hem," Chen cleared his throat. Then he took Brunelle by the elbow. "Why don't we step over here and discuss next steps."

Brunelle looked up sharply, then nodded. He allowed Chen to lead him toward the street. "Right. Next steps. What are the next steps?"

"The next steps are you stepping away from her while she

does her job," Chen said. "I thought you two were an item or something, but it sure doesn't seem like it now."

Brunelle shrugged. "I think maybe we were going to be, but I haven't followed up. I don't like what happened on the Karpati case. I don't want to let that happen again."

Chen looked over his shoulder at Anderson. She had pulled on her latex gloves and was palpating the corpse's neck. "I'm pretty sure she can take care of herself."

Brunelle looked too. He sighed. "Yeah, I know."

"Maybe this has more to do with you," Chen started, but before he could say more, Anderson stood up and stepped over to them.

"No mysteries here," she announced as she pulled her gloves off. "Two stab wounds. One to the stomach, ruptured his small intestine. That would have been survivable, with prompt medical intervention, but the second one was directly to his heart. I'll need to do a full autopsy to determine where exactly it struck, but he was dead as soon as the blade went in."

"Sounds intentional," Brunelle replied.

"Maybe even premeditated," Anderson answered. "Murder one?"

Brunelle allowed a grin. "That's what we'll charge. Just don't let Larry on the stand. He thinks it's justifiable."

Anderson cocked her head at the detective. The motion sent rain drops cascading off her thick hair. Brunelle wished he hadn't noticed, and pretended the sight didn't send his heart racing.

"Justifiable?" she asked.

Chen shrugged. "Community service killing. Guy was a child molester."

Anderson frowned. She looked back at the body. "Did I say murder? I meant suicide. Obvious suicide."

Brunelle shook his head and laughed. "Great. Lead detective says it's justified and the M.E. says it's suicide. No way I get a conviction now."

"Lighten up," Chen slapped his back. "You need a defendant first anyway. Hopefully one that's even worse that ol' George there."

Just then a patrol officer hurried over to them. "We located the suspect," she announced. "Down on Alaska Way. Still had the blood on his hands. They're taking him to the precinct right now."

Chen turned to Brunelle. "You coming to watch the interrogation?"

"Wouldn't miss it for the world," he answered, both relieved and saddened to have an excuse to escape from Kat.

CHAPTER 2

"Fuck you."

Johnny Quilcene sat defiantly in his plastic chair. He probably would have crossed his arms and leaned back with a grin, but his hands were cuffed behind him so he could only offer a slouch to go with his shit-eating grin.

"Nice language," Chen replied evenly. He was seated opposite Quilcene. Next to him was Emily Lassiter, one of the newer detectives. Normally she did property crimes, but it was three in the morning and it was a murder. All hands on deck. Good experience for her and someone to play bad cop to Chen's good.

"Let me explain a few things to you, Johnny," Chen went on. "Then maybe we can reach an understanding."

"Fuck you," Quilcene repeated. The grin turned into a scowl. Almost menacing, Brunelle thought as he watched the proceedings through an obvious two-way mirror with the adjoining room.

Quilcene was young. Nineteen. Shaved head with a bit of black stubble showing. Thin, but wiry. And a nose that wasn't exactly big, but came to a pronounced point. He had tattoos up both arms and some script Brunelle couldn't quite make out crawling around his neck. There was no teardrop tattoo yet—the badge of honor for murderers—but Brunelle had no doubt he'd earned himself one a few hours earlier. The most important tattoo was the one they couldn't see, but was on the information sheet from his last booking: "NGB" across his chest. Native Gangster Blood. He was a member of the Blood gang, a set that was exclusively Native American and centered primarily around the Puyallup tribe near Tacoma. The same tribe George 'Child Molester' Traver was a member of.

"Right," Chen replied. "Fuck you too. Now, let's get to it…"

Quilcene jerked his head at Chen's reply. Chen had his attention. *Good.*

"We know Traver was a dirt bag," Chen continued. "Honestly, between you, me, and the wall, I'm glad he's gone. One less child rapist I gotta track down and waste a jail bed on, ya know? So really, I'm just looking to wrap this up. He had three active warrants, including some pretty sick stuff. I dunno, maybe you knew this guy. Knew he was a child molester, and maybe worse. Maybe he comes at you in the dark and you figure he's gonna rape you too. I dunno. But maybe you pull out that nice little knife you left behind—"

"With your fingerprints," Lassiter interrupted.

"You don't got no fingerprints back yet, bitch," Quilcene sneered. "Those fingerprint dudes are fat fuckers sitting at a desk all day. I seen 'em testify before. They ain't up at three in the fucking morning checking no fucking fingerprints."

Brunelle smiled. Quilcene was an asshole, but he was right.

Lassiter bristled, but Chen kept going.

"She's just saying what we all know. There's probably prints on that knife handle, and if there are, they're probably yours. And Johnny, that's bad news for you."

"And bad news for you if no fingerprints come back," Quilcene countered. "Why don't we just wait and see what bullshit evidence you think you got on me before you start saying you got my fingerprints on the fucking murder weapon and shit."

Chen rubbed his chin. "Well, that's just it, Johnny. Waiting is bad for you."

"Really bad," Lassiter tried. She was new to the game. It was showing.

Brunelle rolled his eyes and hoped Chen could overcome Lassiter's rookie performance.

Quilcene shifted in his seat. His eyes darted from Chen to Lassiter and back again. He was clearly thinking, but he wasn't saying anything.

"Waiting is bad for you," Chen repeated. "This is your chance, Johnny. Your one chance to come clean and tell us your side of the story.

At that, a grin replaced the concern that was starting to show on Quilcene's face. "Naw, I got plenty a' time to tell you my side a' the story. Like, after you give my lawyer all the police reports and I see what you actually got on me and my lawyer finds all the holes in your case."

Brunelle had to nod begrudgingly. The kid knew how the game was played.

"Now, look, Quilcene," Lassiter started. She leaned onto the table and jabbed a finger at him. Her straw-colored hair was pulled back in a simple pony-tail. She might have looked like a simple angry schoolteacher, except for the .45 semi-auto on her hip.

Before she could say more, though, Chen gently pushed down her accusatory finger and nodded congenially to his subject.

"Well, Johnny," he said. "You could do that. But let me tell you why that's a bad idea."

Lassiter yanked her hand out from under Chen's and shot him a narrowed-eye glare. Chen wasn't letting her play her role. Brunelle wondered if she'd be able to let the affront go and channel her 'bad cop' again later if it were needed. He hadn't really dealt with her before—just a nod in the hallway a couple of times. If she was good, she'd be doing homicides soon enough. Best to get to know her now. So Brunelle had two subjects to study through the mirror.

"First off," Chen pointed to a finger on his left hand, "we all know you did it."

Quilcene started to protest, but Chen raised a hand to quiet him. "Now, now. Just hear me out. You don't have to agree with me or confess to anything. Just listen. You did it. You stabbed him. Even if you don't admit that right now, it's important to keep in mind that you did do it and the evidence is almost certainly going to show that."

"Almost," Quilcene laughed. "You said almost. See, man, even you know you ain't got shit."

Chen nodded. "No, right now, I ain't got shit. But I will. Which is why you better get real smart, real fast. That knife may or may not have fingerprints on it, but if it does, we both know they're yours."

Quilcene shrugged and looked away. "Whatever, dude."

"And there are witnesses, Johnny," Chen continued. "They may or may not be able to pick the killer out of a photomontage, but if they can, we both know they're gonna pick you."

"Bunch a' homeless drunks," Quilcene dismissed them with another shrug.

"And Johnny," Chen allowed himself a small smile, "you had blood on your hands. They swabbed your hands when they arrested you. You know, those big Q-tip things? Those are going to the crime lab, and unless you cut yourself on a fucking bottle cap, that blood's gonna come back as George Traver's. No maybes about it."

Quilcene narrowed his eyes at Chen as thoughts raced unexpressed behind them.

"When that happens, Johnny," Lassiter interrupted, "you're going down for murder."

Okay, Brunelle nodded, *that kind of worked. Good job, Lassiter.*

"Unless," Chen raised a finger, but then let the thought linger, unexpressed.

Quilcene just sat there, but his eyes started to get shifty. Experienced detectives like Chen knew that people hate silence. They'll fill it themselves if they have to. Chen was waiting for Quilcene to blurt something out. Brunelle hoped Lassiter knew enough to stay quiet too.

Finally, Quilcene bit. "Unless what?"

Chen grinned. "Unless you come clean now. Before the fingerprints. Before the photomontage. Before the blood. Before you read those police reports with your lawyer and realize we've got your ass and so you better make up some bullshit story to fit the evidence. Juries aren't stupid, Johnny. They see right through that shit."

Brunelle wasn't as sure about juries not being stupid, but he always tried to help them see through the bullshit stories.

"But," Chen wrapped up his sales pitch, "if you tell us your side of the story now, the jury will know you were telling the truth. Hell, the prosecutor will know you're telling the truth, and maybe this never gets to a jury."

"How the fuck does murder not go to a jury?" Quilcene snapped, an incredulous frown on his face.

"When it's not a murder," Chen answered. "Murder is an *unlawful* killing, Johnny. But self defense is a justified killing. It's not murder. Hell, it's not even manslaughter. It's excusable homicide. You just walk."

Brunelle winced. He understood what Chen was trying to do: trick Quilcene into admitting he was the one who'd shoved that knife into Traver's chest. That would solve the 'whodunit?' part of the case. But Brunelle was still uneasy with coaching Quilcene how to cash in a 'get out of jail free' card. He tried to take solace in the fact that a nineteen year old gang-banger would have trouble claiming self defense against a fifty-two-year-old drunk homeless man.

Quilcene pursed his lips and nodded. He didn't say anything for several seconds. Then he looked Chen right in the eye. "You know what kind of sick asshole he was, man?"

Chen nodded. "We sure do. Child molester. Registered sex offender. Active warrants. A real bad guy."

"Yeah," Quilcene sneered. "Real bad guy. Fucker molested half the kids on my block growing up. Finally went to prison, but got out again and moved right back into my neighborhood. We didn't want his sick pervert ass in our neighborhood, but the cops— fuckers like you who're supposed to protect us—the cops said they couldn't do nothing. Level three fucking child molester in a neighborhood full of fucking kids and you fuckers can't do nothing."

"Did he molest one of the kids in your neighborhood, Johnny?" Lassiter asked. 'Bad cop' was long gone. This was genuinely concerned cop. Brunelle wondered if she had young kids. "Is that why you confronted him?"

Quilcene narrowed his eyes again. "Fucker deserved to die. I'm glad he's dead."

"And...?" Chen encouraged.

"And fuck you," Quilcene answered. "I ain't saying shit

more. Fucker deserved it."

Chen leaned back and nodded. "Maybe so. But that's not how the system works."

"Then fuck the system, man," Quilcene practically shouted.

Chen looked to Lassiter then at Quilcene. "You got anything else to say, Johnny?"

"Nope. Fucker deserved it. That's all I got to say. Fucker deserved it. *You* got anything to say?"

Chen stood up. "Yep. You're under arrest for the murder of George Traver."

Brunelle was relieved Quilcene hadn't gone with Chen's suggestion of a self-defense story. 'Fucker deserved it' wasn't an actual legal defense. It might be true, but Brunelle would be able to give the jury the whole 'no one gets to be judge, jury, and executioner' line. It was clichéd but it was true. Still...

He watched as Chen and Lassiter led Quilcene from the interrogation room.

"Fucker deserved it," Quilcene said one last time.

Maybe he did, Brunelle thought. And despite the law, he knew the jury would sympathize. *Damn it.*

CHAPTER 3

Brunelle considered typing 'fucker deserved it' into the search box on the legal research website, but opted for 'justifiable homicide child molester' instead. He clicked the 'search' button and waited while the program scoured the applicable case law.

He'd come in early after only three hours of sleep—a nap, really—to review the available evidence and draft the charging documents. He knew they were going to charge one count of Murder in the First Degree, but he also knew they didn't quite have the evidence yet. Quilcene roughly matched the suspect description and was arrested in the area with blood on his hands, but it had been less than twelve hours since the murder. The 'fat fuckers' in the fingerprint unit were just getting to work; it'd be at least until the afternoon, if not tomorrow, before they confirmed the match. The DNA on Traver's blood would take at least a day longer than that, even with a 'drop everything' rush. And detectives still had to go back out to show photomontages to the witnesses from the night before—if they could find even them, and if they weren't too drunk to remember.

So instead of filing charges, he'd have to ask the judge to agree that there was 'probable cause' to believe Quilcene had committed the crime, and then hold him for seventy-two hours while the evidence caught up with the arrest. Then he could come in and file charges with confidence. It would also give him three days to research, and rebut, the 'fucker deserved it' defense.

The search was done and Brunelle clicked on the first case in the list, but before he could begin reading it, there was a knock on his doorframe.

It was Matt Duncan, the elected prosecutor for King County. Brunelle's boss. Everyone's boss.

"Have you filed charges against Quilcene yet?" he asked.

Brunelle shook his head. "Not yet. We're waiting on some lab results so I'm going to ask for a seventy-two hour hold."

Duncan nodded. "Good. Hold off. We need to talk."

Brunelle didn't like the sound of that. He didn't need Duncan buying off on the 'fucker deserved it' bit. "What is it?"

Duncan grimaced. "Why don't you come to my office? There's a …" He paused, seeking the right word. "A complication."

"That doesn't sound good," Brunelle said as he stood from his chair.

Duncan offered a shrug and a smile. "I learned a long time ago to think of every difficulty as an opportunity."

Brunelle followed him down the hall to his corner office. "How big is this 'opportunity'?"

Duncan turned back as they reached his office door. "Pretty big."

Duncan's office boasted a panoramic view of Elliot Bay, albeit between the other, taller buildings closer to the waterfront. Still, it was a nice view and the furniture was set up to allow visitors to enjoy it as they sat at the large conference table that took up half of the oversized office.

Brunelle sat down and immediately noticed a leather-bound

book laying open at the center of the table. He pulled it to him and tipped it closed long enough to read the spine: 'Indian Treaties of the Northwest Territories.'

He looked up at Duncan. "Big, huh?"

Duncan was gazing out the window, his hands clasped behind his back. "Yeah. Big." He turned around and sat opposite Brunelle. "I just got off the phone with the lawyer for the Puyallup Indian Tribe, down by Tacoma. She called me about the Puyallup Tribal Court. Did you know they had a court?"

"I didn't even know they had a lawyer."

Duncan laughed. "Yep. A lawyer—several, in fact—a judge, and a court. And apparently that court was created pursuant to their treaty with the United States government."

Brunelle looked down again at the tome in his hand. "I don't like where this is going," he said. "Quilcene is Native Gangster Blood. They're starting to come up to Seattle. So I know he's Native. Is he Puyallup?"

"Exactly," Duncan sighed. "And so is your victim. George something, right?"

"Traver."

"Right. George Traver. They're both Puyallup Indians."

"Native American," Brunelle corrected.

"What?" Duncan cocked his head at Brunelle.

"Native American," Brunelle repeated. "I don't think we're supposed to say 'Indian' any more."

Duncan frowned. "Their lawyer did. She specifically said 'Puyallup Indian Tribe,'"

"Yeah, it's different when you say it that way, I think." Brunelle looked at the ceiling as he considered. "It's officially the Puyallup Indian Tribe, but you refer to the members of it as Native American, or even just Native."

"Really?"

Brunelle shrugged. "I think so."

Duncan smiled. "I knew you were the right man for the job."

Brunelle leaned back in his chair and crossed his arms. "Crap. What job?"

Duncan suppressed a friendly laugh. "Remember that treaty I mentioned? The one in that book you're trying to ignore right now?"

Brunelle raised an indignant eyebrow. "I'm not trying to ignore anything. In fact, I snuck a peek at the title when you were gazing importantly out the window."

"Well, go ahead and take it," Duncan said. "You're going to want to brush up on Indian Law. Er, sorry, Native American Law."

Brunelle slid the book to the side. "Enough riddles, Matt. What's going on?"

Duncan smiled again, creasing his eyes playfully. "Apparently, that treaty gives the Tribe jurisdiction over crimes committed by one tribal member against another. That's why their lawyer called. To assert that treaty right."

Brunelle ran a hand through his closely cropped hair. "Are you fucking kidding me? I've never heard of anything like that. The murder happened in our county. We have jurisdiction."

"I guess not," Duncan replied. "Their lawyer explained it pretty convincingly. It gives them original jurisdiction to any crime committed by one tribal member against the other."

"Then why hasn't this ever come up before?"

"Turns out, it has," Duncan answered. "About a hundred years ago, right after the treaty was signed. The Tribe asserted the treaty right, but the federal court basically invalidated it. Held that the provision only applied to conduct exclusively on the reservation and not otherwise prohibited by state or federal law."

"Well, I'd say murder is otherwise prohibited by state law," Brunelle pointed out.

"Of course it is," Duncan agreed. "But it was a bullshit decision. The treaty doesn't say anything of the sort. It was just a racist ruling by a federal government that never honored any treaty with any tribe."

Brunelle raised an eyebrow at his boss's impassioned description.

"Their lawyer's words," he explained. "Not mine."

Brunelle nodded. "Of course."

"But it doesn't matter," Duncan went on. "They're asserting the treaty now, and the Bureau of Indian Affairs—or Native American Affairs, or whatever—is backing them. We have no choice."

"You could cite that racist decision as precedent," Brunelle suggested unhelpfully.

Duncan shook his head. "I don't need that kind of press."

"Matt, listen to me." Brunelle leaned forward earnestly. "You can't send a murder case to some rinky-dink tribal court. Do they even have a prosecutor?"

"They do now." Duncan stuck out a hand to shake. "Congratulations."

Brunelle slumped back in his chair and put his hand over his face. "Are you fucking kidding me?"

Duncan shook his head. "Afraid not, Dave. No joke. You're going to be our emissary to the Puyallup Tribal Court." Then he looked at his watch. "Oh, shit. You'd better get going. Your co-counsel is expecting you at ten-thirty."

Brunelle peeked through his fingers. "Co-counsel?"

CHAPTER 4

Brunelle took exit 135 off southbound Interstate 5 and hoped there would be signs for 'Puyallup Tribal Court.' His GPS had no address for it and he didn't have a phone number to call to ask for directions. Duncan's 'Look for the casino' had been unhelpful as well, although he realized as he reached the end of the off-ramp and confirmed no signs for the court, that he really had no option but to turn left under the freeway and head for the casino complex that dominated the immediate area.

The tribal lands sat on the curve where the aptly named River Road turned from its course parallel to the Puyallup River to head south into downtown Tacoma. As it was originally designed to bypass, and not service, the reservation, someone coming from the direction of Tacoma, and unfamiliar with the local roads—like Brunelle just then—could quickly find himself rounding a sharp bend onto River Road and speeding away from the tribal land.

Brunelle had spotted what looked like some sort of administrative building north of the casino but when he turned onto River Road, and before he could do anything about, it he found himself heading the wrong way, and fast.

He desperately turned onto the only side street before River Road transformed into a state highway leading into rural Pierce County. He found himself driving up a steep hill, with a long brick wall on his right and nothing but a steep, tree-filled drop-off to his left. When he reached the top, the road leveled out onto a residential street with a breath-taking view of Mt. Rainier. He pulled over to get his bearings in front of an old craftsman on a double lot with a 'For Sale' sign out front.

He wondered whether he'd completely left the reservation. He got his answer when he looked around and saw a large sign across the street from the craftsman: 'Puyallup Tribal Cemetery.' He looked again at the craftsman.

"Good luck selling that," he murmured, wondering who would ever live across the street from an Indian burial ground.

He turned the car onto the side street between the house and the graveyard and headed down the back of the hill toward what he hoped was that administration building he'd seen. He knew he was getting closer when the road signs were suddenly in both English and that Native American alphabet the Northwest tribes had adapted from the Latin letters. He especially liked the question mark thing without the dot.

A quick right onto another side street, then a slow left into a parking lot and Brunelle was pulling his car into the parking stall directly in front of the administrative building he'd seen. The sign out front read simply, 'Puyallup Indian Tribe.'

"Whew, made it." He put it in park and turned off the engine. Then he realized he still didn't know where the court was located, let alone the prosecutor's office.

~*~

Brunelle stepped into the lobby of the administration building and immediately noticed the cubicle to his right. The woman there sat behind one of those elevated countertops that suggested visitors should check in with her. So he did.

"Hello." He tried to sound like he wanted to be there. "Could you direct me to the prosecutor's office?"

The woman, who had been doing some task on her computer, looked up at him like she was really tired of visitors always checking in with her. She was heavy-set with her black hair pulled into a ponytail, and was wearing the type of top he would have expected to see on a pediatric nurse. Brunelle supposed she was Native, but thought she might be Hispanic. Maybe both. Or Hawaiian. He tried not to shrug.

"Prosecutor's office?" the woman repeated. "You mean the Pierce County Prosecutor's Office? That's downtown." She pointed vaguely toward the direction of downtown Tacoma.

"Er, no," Brunelle answered. "The tribal prosecutor's office.

The confusion on the woman's face deepened. "Tribal prosecutor? Hey, Janie!" She craned her neck to see around Brunelle. "Do we have a tribal prosecutor?"

A woman's head popped up from behind a cubicle wall on the opposite side of the small lobby. She looked like any other middle-aged lady walking down the street. "The Tribe has a lawyer, but that's for other stuff. Suing people and staying compliant with codes and stuff. Our cases get filed into the county prosecutor's office."

The first woman looked back at Brunelle. "Yeah, sorry. We don't have a prosecutor."

Brunelle was about to argue with her when the other woman shouted over her cubicle wall again. "Wait! Are you here on that murder case?"

Now we're getting somewhere, Brunelle thought. "Yes, I'm Dave Bru—"

"Murder case?!" the first woman interjected. "We had a murder here?"

"Not exactly," Brunelle started.

"No, no," interrupted the cubicle woman. "One of our tribe members murdered another one up in Seattle and the tribe is gonna prosecute him. I heard about it from Kelly this morning."

"Wow," the first lady said. "We *are* going to need a prosecutor then." She looked at Brunelle. "Are you the defense attorney?"

"No," he replied quickly, trying to control his growing impatience. "I'm the prosecutor."

The woman crossed her arms. "I thought you were looking for the prosecutor?"

Brunelle could feel his blood pressure starting to rise. "I am. I'm from the King County—"

"Police," cubicle woman said.

"No, no, no." Brunelle ran a hand down his face. "Not the King County Police. First of all, it's the King County *Sheriff*, not 'police.' Second, I'm—"

"No," the woman interrupted. "The police station. Go to the police station. That's where Kelly works."

"Who's Kelly?" Brunelle asked.

Cubicle woman rolled her eyes and sighed audibly. "She's the one who told me about the murder. Don't you listen?"

Brunelle closed his eyes and counted to three. He didn't think he'd make it to ten. "Where's the police station, please?"

The first woman seemed eager for him to leave as well. "Go back outside, turn left, and it's two doors down. Says 'Puyallup Tribal Police' on the door."

"Thanks," Brunelle nodded and forced a smile. He stepped through the doors and paused to get his bearings. As the door closed behind him, he heard cubicle woman ask her friend, "I wonder who he was anyway?"

Brunelle took a deep, cleansing breath and looked at his watch. 10:32. He was late now too. Things were going great so far.

Two doors down was indeed the lobby to the Puyallup Tribal Police station. Stepping inside, Brunelle decided to postpone asking where the tribal prosecutor was until after he'd introduced himself by both name and title.

"Hello," he said to the uniformed young woman behind the bullet proof glass. "I'm Dave Brunelle from the King County Prosecutor's Office. I was supposed to meet with someone at ten-thirty regarding a murder by one tribal member against another up in Seattle last night."

The officer listened, nodded, then stood up and disappeared from view. After several seconds, the only interior door in the lobby buzzed and the officer opened it from the inside with a loud clack.

"Freddy's in the last room on the right," she informed Brunelle as he stepped through the door into a tightly packed cubicle maze.

"Freddy?" he asked.

The officer smiled. "Our prosecutor." She made quote marks in the air with her fingers when she said the word 'prosecutor.'

Great, Brunelle thought. "Thanks," he said.

Freddy was indeed in the last room on the right. As near as Brunelle could tell, it was a combination file room, junk room, and discarded furniture room. Freddy stood in the corner of it, apparently trying to make some order out of it. And also because there didn't seem to be any chairs. None that weren't obviously broken anyway.

"Mr. Brunelle!" Freddy called out. He rushed over to shake Brunelle's hand. He was about ten years younger than Brunelle—in his early thirties—and at least fifty pounds heavier, which was even more noticeable since he was a good six inches shorter too. His skin was a deep tone, not as dark as the Native/Hispanic/Hawaiian receptionist, but darker than Brunelle's pink pastel. Thick eyebrows and a disarming smile completed the look. He grabbed Brunelle's hand and pumped it enthusiastically. "It's an honor to meet you. Thank you for helping us out on this case."

"Uh, sure," Brunelle replied, extracting his hand. "Glad to help, I guess. Uh, what did you say your name was?"

"Ha, right." Freddy winked and pointed a gun-shaped finger at Brunelle. "Freddy. Freddy McCloud."

Brunelle nodded. "Nice to meet you." Then he noticed Freddy McCloud wasn't even wearing a tie. He started to feel a bit overdressed in his suit and overcoat.

"Man, this is gonna be great." Freddy rubbed his hands together. "I'm so glad we got a real prosecutor on our side. Now I can just pop some popcorn and watch the show."

Brunelle demurred. "Well, I'll try to live up."

Freddy laughed and shook his head. "No, not you," he said. "Talon."

Brunelle's eyebrows knitted together. "Talon? Who's Talon?"

Freddy's grin blossomed into full blown smile. "She's the defense attorney. And she's gonna kick your ass."

CHAPTER 5

Before Brunelle could figure out how to respond, Freddy slapped his forehead.

"Oh, man! We're late." He rushed around the table and tugged Brunelle's arm as he passed. "We don't want to piss him off."

Brunelle staggered after Freddy as he disappeared into the hallway. "Piss who off? And what are we late for? I thought I was meeting you at ten-thirty."

"No, we're late for the status conference," Freddy yelled over the cubicles he was racing through. "And the judge. We don't want to piss off Judge LeClair. Not again."

"Again?" Brunelle shook his head. "But I just got here."

~*~

The courtroom was back in the main part of the administration building. Brunelle made sure to say "Hi" to the sort-of-receptionist as he walked through the lobby, trying to keep up with Freddy, who was half-running and muttering something Brunelle couldn't quite hear. After a couple of turns down a couple of hallways, Freddy threw open a random door and disappeared inside. A second later, as Brunelle reached the door, Freddy stuck his head back out into the hallway.

"In here," he announced.

"I figured," Brunelle replied, even as Freddy slipped back out of sight.

Brunelle took a moment to read the sign on the door: 'Judge's Chambers.' It already looked more official than Freddy's 'office.' Brunelle composed himself, stood up straight, and walked inside.

"You're late."

Brunelle managed a contrite nod to the man seated behind the large desk in the center of the far wall. "My apologies, Your Honor. I didn't even know I was going to be here this morning, let alone late for anything. I'm still playing catch-up."

The judge didn't stand up from his desk; he just scanned Brunelle through narrowed eyes. He was youngish—probably the same early forty-something as Brunelle—with a full head of disheveled black hair. There was no mistaking his Native ancestry. High cheek bones, sharp nose, and wise wrinkles in the corners of his bronze skin.

"Lateness shows disrespect," he said. "Do not disrespect me, Mr. Brunelle."

Brunelle offered another conciliatory nod. "Yes, Your Honor."

"When you disrespect me, you disrespect my court," LeClair went on.

"Yes, Your Honor," Brunelle agreed.

"When you disrespect my court, you disrespect my people."

"Yes, Your Honor."

"Do not disrespect my people, Mr. Brunelle."

"Yes, Your Honor."

LeClair waited a moment, eyeing Brunelle, then turned to look at Freddy. Brunelle supposed LeClair knew it was Freddy's fault they were late. He took some solace in that. Anyway, it wasn't about being late; it was about being an outsider. It was about being a big shot prosecutor from the biggest city the state—one named after a Native chief, but they couldn't even show enough respect to spell it right. His name was Sealth, not Seattle.

Under different circumstances, Brunelle might have enjoyed a discussion about respecting cultural traditions and the historical interaction between European and Native peoples in the Pacific Northwest.

Actually, he wouldn't have enjoyed it. But he probably could have tolerated it.

But these weren't different circumstances. These were the usual circumstances. Judge and lawyer. LeClair was the judge and he was the lawyer. Angry judges rule against lawyers who make them angry. And judges who feel respected rule in favor of lawyers who show them respect.

Brunelle thought LeClair was about to offer him the slightest smile to acknowledge Brunelle's response to his test. But instead, Brunelle was pushed to the side by the woman who marched into the room.

"Sorry I'm late, Judge. Got caught in a deposition. And then there was no parking. Some jackass in a Ford took my usual spot so I had to park all the way over at the casino and walk."

It was Talon. Brunelle knew.

He didn't know if it was her first name, or her last name, or her nickname. It didn't matter. It was the perfect name.

She was Talon.

And she was stunning.

Long, straight, silky black hair hung to the middle of her athletic back. She wore a red silk blouse and gray skirt, just tight and just short enough to be attractive and professional at the same time. Dark stockings and high heels that were almost, but not quite, stilettos. And her face—a perfect, Native American angel.

A goddess, Brunelle thought. *Uh, if they have those.*

He flashed his best smile and extended a hand in greeting. He wanted to come across as smooth, despite the blood pounding in his ears.

"Hello," he crooned. Then, when she just stared at him and his hand, he tried, "I'm the jackass."

No reaction. Not a smile. Not a wince. Nothing. Just coal black eyes staring right though him.

"Er, the Ford," Brunelle stammered. "I'm the jackass who took your parking space. Sorry about that."

Talon still just stared at him, but Freddy jumped up to commence the introductions.

"Talon Winter, this is Dave Brunelle. He's a King County homicide prosecutor. Dave, this is Talon Winter, she's—"

"I," Talon interrupted, "am going to kick your ass." For the first time her face showed an emotion other than stunned contempt. There was a gleam in her eye and a smile hidden in the corner of her mouth. She looked down at Brunelle's still-extended hand just long enough for him to know she wasn't going to shake it.

Brunelle lowered it finally. He'd have to work harder for physical contact.

"Nice to meet you too," he answered. "You represent the murderer, I take it?"

A little needling to see how she'd react.

"I represent Mr. Quilcene," she corrected. Then she extracted some papers from her shoulder-strapped brief case. "Which is how you will refer to him as well. At least in open court."

Brunelle nodded slowly, acknowledging the statement but not agreeing to it. He managed not to give voice to his simple thought: complete shrew.

"We'll see about that," he replied. He pointed to her pleadings. "Are those your motions *in limine* already? Most defense attorneys I know wait until the last minute to file all their motions to limit what I can or can't say."

"I'm not most defense attorneys," Talon hissed. "And you don't know me."

Brunelle felt a rush of conflicting emotions as he considered wanting to know her. "We haven't even had the arraignment yet," he pointed out.

"I'm always several steps ahead. You're going to learn that, Mr. Jackass."

Brunelle realized that wouldn't be the last time she called him that. Such was his reward for trying to be funny.

"Be careful," he warned. "Several steps ahead is fine—unless the bridge collapses under your feet."

Talon narrowed her eyes and cocked her head. It sent her hair swinging in a silky waterfall against her shining blouse. Brunelle cinched his own eyes against the intoxicating sight, and turned instead to look at the judge, who was sitting quietly, enjoying the show.

"So, Mr. McCloud said we're having a status conference?" Brunelle asked the judge.

"'Mr. McCloud'?" Talon laughed. "Listen to your big shot partner, Freddy. He thinks you're a real lawyer."

Freddy kept his smile plastered to his face, but it left his eyes. Brunelle was about to say something in his defense when the judge finally decided to take control.

"Yes, Mr. Brunelle. This is a status conference. I want to discuss all preliminary matters before formal initiation of the criminal case."

Brunelle shrugged. It wasn't what he was used to, but he

could see the value in it. "All right, Your Honor." He sat down in one of the two chairs opposite the judge. "Where shall we start?"

Talon waited a moment, then pulled the other chair a few inches away from Brunelle and sat down. Freddy leaned against the wall.

Talon handed Brunelle and LeClair each a copy of her pleadings. "These are my initial motions *in limine.* They outline how the case should proceed," she explained, as if she were the judge, not just one of the litigants. She extracted more papers from her bag and shoved them at Brunelle and the judge.

Judge LeClair simply started a stack on top of the thin file folder he had centered on his desktop. Brunelle let them lay where Talon set them. He would look at them as the judge might instruct him to.

Freddy, though, leaned in long enough to grab the top document off of Brunelle's stack and start thumbing loudly through it.

Talon listed the titles of her pleadings. "Motion to suppress identification. Motion to suppress physical evidence. Affirmative defenses. Motion to dismiss…"

After several more, Judge LeClair lifted his hand to stop her. "Thank you, Ms. Winter. I shall review these right away. The arraignment will take place tomorrow morning. That will give our officers time to transport Mr. Quilcene to our court."

"I might need one more day, Your Honor," Brunelle interjected. "I'm still waiting on some lab results."

"Do you mean to tell me, Mr. Brunelle," Judge LeClair raised an eyebrow at him, "that you are holding a member of my tribe without enough evidence to charge him?"

Brunelle offered a polite smile. "Of course not, Your Honor. Tomorrow morning will be fine. Thank you."

"Good," the judge replied sharply. "We will conduct a bail hearing as well and schedule the trial date. The trial will commence within sixty days, no longer."

LeClair looked at Brunelle to see if he would protest. Murder trials were routinely scheduled a year or more after arraignment. But Brunelle had learned not to argue with this judge. Not right then, anyway. If there were a legitimate basis to delay the trial—and there almost always was—he could raise it later.

"Motions to suppress," LeClair went on, "must be filed by the pre-trial conference, which will be in one month."

"I've already filed mine, Your Honor," Talon chirped. She leaned forward to tap once on the judge's pile.

The judge smiled at her, a truly warm smile. He then turned to Brunelle as if to make sure he'd seen it. He had.

"Also by pre-trial," Judge LeClair continued, "the prosecution will hand over all evidence in its possession which it intends to use at trial, and the defendant will disclose the nature of his defense."

Brunelle was about to point out that homicide investigations routinely turned up additional evidence even after the arrest and arraignment of the defendant, but Talon spoke up first.

"I've already filed notice of our defense," she practically sang. She looked at Brunelle. For the first time, she smiled at him. The kind of smile a tiger might give its prey before killing it.

"You have?" Judge LeClair asked. He started to look through his stack of papers.

"She sure did." Freddy stepped forward, one hand gripping a crumpled pleading, the other stuffed into his hair. "And it's brilliant!"

CHAPTER 6

Brunelle snatched the paper out of Freddy's hand and scanned the page.

"'Blood revenge'?" he read aloud. "What the hell type of defense is that?"

"It's a type justifiable homicide," Freddy answered. He pointed at Talon's pleading. "It says so right there."

Brunelle squeezed his eyes shut for a moment. When he opened them, he stared right at Talon. "Blood revenge?"

"Blood revenge," she grinned.

"Blood revenge," the judge repeated slowly, obviously trying the idea on for size. And obviously liking it.

Brunelle shook his head.

"Sometimes," Talon beamed, "being several steps ahead means you've reached the other side when the bridge collapses under your opponent's feet."

~*~

"Revenge?" Chen asked across his desk. "How is that a defense? It's a reason—maybe a good one—but it's not a defense."

"Well, not just revenge," Brunelle answered, leaning back in the chair opposite the detective. "Blood revenge. It's an old Indian tradition, I guess. Kind of an honor killing."

"Honor killing?" It was Kat. She'd suddenly appeared in Chen's doorway, bearing reports. "Isn't that when they stone some girl to death because her uncle molested her?"

Brunelle stood up awkwardly, shaken by Kat's unexpected appearance. Then he was irritated at himself for being so obvious about his surprise. "Er, I don't know. Maybe. But here, they killed the molester."

Kat raised an eyebrow. "Oh, yeah?" She threw the reports on Chen's desk without comment.

Chen glanced at them and offered a nod of thanks.

"Um. Yeah," Brunelle went on. He wished he weren't so uncomfortable around her. She seemed to feed off it somehow. She leveled a glance at him both inviting and ice cold. "That murder in Pioneer Square, remember? Our victim was a child molester."

"Oh, right," Kat smiled. "The suicide."

"Blood revenge," Chen corrected. "Apparently that's a defense."

Kat glanced sideways at Brunelle. "Oh, really?" she practically threatened. "That's good to know."

Brunelle shook his head. "No, sorry, it's only available to Native Americans, and it has to be something more than some guy just not calling you."

"What makes you think I'm not Native?" Kat put her hands on her hips. "And what makes you think I care that you haven't called me?"

Brunelle's eyes narrowed against her unexpected questions. He decided to ignore them for the moment and press on with his explanation. "They're claiming that since the tribal court's jurisdiction comes from a hundred-and-fifty-year-old treaty, they get to raise a hundred-and-fifty-year-old defenses. Apparently, the way blood revenge worked, if you killed someone in another tribe, then that other tribe could kill someone from your tribe."

Chen frowned. "Did Traver kill someone?"

Brunelle threw his hands wide. "Thank you! No, he didn't. So the defense shouldn't even be available."

"What did he do?" Kat asked.

Brunelle rubbed the back of his neck. "Ah, well... He diddled the defendant's niece."

Kat's face hardened. "Yep. Not guilty. Easy verdict."

"Yep. You're not on my jury. Easy decision," Brunelle parroted. "The lead detective and the medical examiner both on the side of the defendant. This trial should go great."

"So don't call us as witnesses." Kat winked at Chen.

"I'm pretty sure I have to," Brunelle complained. "You, at least. Somebody's gotta tell the jury how Traver died."

Kat nodded. "Good point. Well, just keep it short and sweet. Is he dead? Yep. Somebody stab him? Yep. No further questions."

Brunelle surrendered a weak grin. "Yeah, that'll be great... until cross exam. When the defense attorney gets you to tell the jury the bastard deserved it."

Brunelle sighed as he remembered Talon. How she was already three steps ahead of him. How she called him a jackass. How she looked in that red blouse.

"What's he like?" Kat asked.

The question shook Brunelle from his thoughts. "Who?"

"The defense attorney," Kat clarified. "What's he like?"

"Oh, um," Brunelle stammered. "Pretty good, I think. I've never met her before, but she seemed pretty damn prepared at that stupid status conference."

Brunelle tried to hide his thoughts by glancing out Chen's

window.

Kat paused. "She?"

"Hm?" Brunelle turned back from the window but didn't quite look at her.

"The defense attorney is a woman?"

"Um, yeah," Brunelle nodded. "I guess so."

Kat laughed. "'I guess so,' he says."

Chen stood up. "I'm going to go look for a report or something. I'll be back a long time from now."

"Coward," Brunelle teased.

"Takes one to know one," Chen whispered as he slipped into the hallway.

Kat crossed her arms and just stared at Brunelle for several seconds. He could feel himself flushing under her gaze. He tried not to think of Talon's hair.

"She's totally hot, isn't she?" Kat demanded.

"No," Brunelle replied too loudly and too quickly. "No. Not at all."

Kat cocked her head. "I'm going to see her when I testify, dummy."

Brunelle ran a hand over his hair. "Oh, right," he sighed. "Okay, yeah. She's a total hottie. Almost beyond description. I can barely think. But, she's also a total bitch. So yeah, totally hot total bitch."

Kat clicked her tongue. "Tsk, tsk, Mr. Brunelle. We finally get a chance to talk and it ends with you telling me how hot some other woman is."

Brunelle finally looked her in the eye. "Why is that how it ends?"

"Because I'm leaving." She gave a last, confirming glance at the reports she'd left on Chen's desk, then turned to leave. "Say 'Hi' to Freddy for me."

"You know Freddy McCloud?" Brunelle asked, the surprise in his voice clear.

"Yep," Kat answered with a grin. "We dated when he was in law school and I was a resident at Tacoma General. Right after Lizzy's dad and I split up."

Brunelle nodded thoughtfully, but didn't say anything.

"He's a really nice guy," Kat went on. "You could learn a thing or two from him."

Then she walked away without another word.

Brunelle shook his head and looked out the window again. His mind raced from Talon to Kat to Freddy to the dead form of George Traver.

"Revenge," he muttered.

CHAPTER 7

Kat's parting words shook Brunelle more than he would have liked to admit. He spent the rest of the afternoon drafting charging documents that normally wouldn't have taken him more than thirty minutes to create. As the day drew to a close and he was satisfied he was prepared for the next morning's arraignment, he picked up the phone and booked a room at the hotel across the street from the casino.

There was no way he was going to risk being late again because of bad traffic or a blocking accident. He was going to be within walking distance, file in hand. He knew when it came time for trial, he'd be spending a couple of weeks down there. Might as well get used to it.

Besides, he could unwind over a beer and blackjack.

Once he was checked in, he walked across the street and took out fifty bucks from the casino's ATM. That would be his limit. Once it was gone, he'd head back to his room.

Three hours later, he still had forty bucks in his wallet and too many beers in his bloodstream.

He stood up from the blackjack table and decided to walk

around the casino for a bit to clear his head. He drained the last of his beer and calculated how long it would be until he felt sober again. He knew from his early days prosecuting DUIs that his body would burn off about one drink an hour.

He looked at his watch. He needed another hour without drinking.

He looked at his empty beer bottle. Or one more beer and two more hours of blackjack.

He sat down at the bar in the center of the cavernous, smoke-filled casino and ordered another beer. Then he ran a hand over his short hair as he tried to figure out why he felt so bad about Kat storming out on him.

He hadn't said anything that wasn't true. Didn't women always say they wanted honesty? And anyway, she'd brought it up, not him. She'd forced the issue. It wasn't his fault Talon was hot; it was Talon's. And anyway, she was a bitch. A shrew. That was one of those words nobody used any more, but it fit perfectly. And weren't shrews supposed to be tamed? Who was going to tame her? Him? Not likely. He was a jackass. And besides, nothing gets a conviction overturned on appeal like the prosecutor sleeping with the defense attorney. Not like that ever happened, but he didn't want to be the first. He didn't need that. He didn't need her either. And he didn't need Kat. Maybe that's why she was so mad, because he hadn't called her, hadn't followed up on what they both felt. Didn't she understand he didn't want to endanger her? Sure, they could have just hooked up, no strings attached, but he knew it wouldn't have stopped there. Maybe that's what he was scared of. Maybe he should just try for another barmaid.

He looked up at the woman serving the drinks.

"Never mind," he muttered. And he was definitely too drunk to drive all the way back up to Seattle before closing time.

"Never mind what?"

Brunelle turned sharply at the voice sitting down next to him. It was Freddy. Freddy, the really nice guy. Always smiling. No wonder Kat liked him. Or had liked him. Or still did.

Brunelle grabbed his forehead. Thinking hurt.

He lowered his hand and shook his head. "Like I said, never mind." Then he returned his partner's smile. "What are you doing here?"

Freddy shrugged and patted his thick gut. "Best food in Tacoma. I had dinner, then stuck around for some slots. I was just heading out when I saw you sitting here."

He looked at Brunelle's hand on his beer and appraised the flush on his face. "You're not driving back up to Seattle tonight, are you?"

Brunelle shook his head. "No. I got a hotel room. I didn't want to be late to old man LeClair's courtroom tomorrow morning.

Freddy spun and faced forward on his barstool. "Good thinking. He's gonna give you shit the whole trial, just because you're not Native. No reason to piss him off extra."

"Hardly seems fair," Brunelle complained. "But I'll deal with it. Lots of judges are jerks for lots of different reasons."

Freddy shrugged. "If you say so. But he's gonna let Talon go to town on her stupid blood revenge defense."

"Stupid?" Brunelle knotted his eyebrows. "I thought you said it was brilliant?"

"It can be both," Freddy grinned. "It's brilliant of Talon to raise it. I mean, really, her guy's guilty as hell. He had blood on his hands, for Christ's sake. So if you can't deny it, justify it. That's brilliant. But it's stupid because that's not how it really worked."

Brunelle cocked his head. "It's not?"

"Nope." Freddy looked straight ahead as he explained, usual

smile lost in a serious expression, hands extended to emphasize his points. "Talon's trying to make blood revenge a judicial remedy. But it wasn't judicial. It was extra-judicial. If someone killed someone in your tribe, then you killed someone in theirs and it was over. No need for the chiefs to get involved. That was the whole point. Self help."

"Okay, but isn't that what Quilcene did?" Brunelle countered.

Freddy shrugged. "Sort of. I don't know. I guess I'm not explaining it very well. I think if you were going to do that, really going to do that, then Talon and LeClair better realize what they're doing. Blood revenge didn't always end it. Remember, how someone killed someone in your family because you killed someone in theirs? Well, guess what? Now someone's killed someone in your family. So you get to kill someone in theirs. Now it's a blood feud. It might never end."

Brunelle nodded. "Good point. Kind of a policy argument. We can argue that blood revenge was a bad idea and—"

Freddy raised a hand. "Oh, I didn't say blood revenge was a bad idea." He turned to Brunelle again, his smile back and on full display. But different somehow. "I think it's a great idea. Just let them handle it. Keep us out of it. Traver molests Quilcene's niece, so Quilcene kills him. Fine. Then someone from Traver's family kills Quilcene or one of his relatives. And we stay the hell out of it."

Brunelle shook his head. "Not gonna happen. Quilcene's in custody and my detective says Traver didn't have any family."

Freddy's smile faded a bit. "Is that right?"

"Yeah," Brunelle answered. "So maybe the blood feud ends here after all."

Freddy looked straight ahead again and nodded. "Yeah, maybe."

The conversation was starting to sober Brunelle up. He slid his beer away. "I think I'm done drinking. Wanna play a few hands of blackjack before calling it a night?"

Freddy was quick to beg off. "No, that's okay." He tapped his hands on the countertop. "Thanks anyway, but I think I'm gonna head out. I've got some things to do. I'll see you in the morning."

"Sounds good," Brunelle patted him on the back as they both stood up. "See you tomorrow."

As Freddy started to walk away, Brunelle felt glad for the relief their shop talk had brought to his melancholic ruminations. But realizing that made him think of Kat again.

"Oh, hey, Freddy!" he called out after him through the casino crowd. "Kat says 'Hi'!"

But Freddy didn't turn around. Apparently, it was too loud in the casino between the ringing slots and the talking patrons. Brunelle watched him walk out to the south parking lot and disappear into the black night.

Brunelle pulled out his wallet and stared at the forty-odd dollars he had left. He scanned the casino and spotted a poker table. Perfect. It would take him no time to lose forty dollars at poker.

~*~

Brunelle stepped out into the south parking lot. It was starting to rain—just a light mist really. The blacktop was glistening and a fine spray tickled his face. He welcomed the sensation. One more thing to wake him up for his walk back to the hotel.

He shook his head at himself. Part of the reason he'd walked to the casino, despite the ever-present threat of rain in the the fall, was the thought—hope?—that Talon might be there and he didn't want to take another one of her usual parking spots. He didn't want her to call him jackass again. Silly how he'd changed his behavior because of a woman he knew he'd never actually be with.

He stuck his hands in his pockets and wondered what was wrong with himself. But just as he began ticking back through past lovers, his thoughts were shattered by a scream.

It sounded like a girl but the voice was a man's. Brunelle knew a man screaming like a girl was bad. Maybe very bad.

He ran in the direction of the scream, toward the grassy strip separating the casino parking lot from the tribe's administration building. He got there at the same time as two other casino patrons who'd also been in the parking lot.

"Step back," Brunelle ordered as they reached the scene. The crime scene, he knew.

A young man, maybe even a teenager, lay on the grass, eyes open and glassy. Large blotches, black in the parking lot lights, stained his shirt—one at his stomach, the other over his heart. Brunelle knelt down and checked for a pulse under the boy's 'NGB' neck tattoo. Nothing.

"He's dead," Brunelle announced.

"That's not the worst of it."

Brunelle jerked his head up to see Freddy standing there, rain dripping from his hair and his chest heaving. He pointed at the victim.

"That's Bobby Quilcene. Johnny's cousin."

CHAPTER 8

An hour later, Brunelle and Freddy were still in the casino parking lot. They were both leaning against a cop car, its lights flashing against the back of their damp heads. Officers from the Tribal Police and the Pierce County Medical Examiner were still investigating the scene across the parking lot, the steady mist unrelenting in the dark.

Brunelle looked at his watch. It was almost 1 a.m. "This still won't give us an excuse to be late, will it?"

Freddy surrendered a tired laugh. "Nope. We'll be exhausted, but we better not be late."

Brunelle nodded. "Well, hopefully they'll get to us soon."

He was used to coming and going from crime scenes at his pleasure. But he didn't know these cops or these M.E.s and he wouldn't be prosecuting this murder. He was just a witness. A cold, tired, wet witness.

Then he realized something.

He turned to Freddy. "Hey, why were you even still around? You left a good half an hour before I did."

"Eh?" Freddy looked over at him, then away again. He

rubbed the back of his wet neck. "Oh, I was just, um, sitting in my car. You know, talking on the phone with, uh, someone."

"Oh," Brunelle nodded. He didn't ask who. Maybe Freddy had heard him shout 'Hi' from Kat after all.

A few quiet minutes later a patrol officer finally made his way over to them. They'd already been separated once to give their initial verbal statements. This cop had some blank-lined statement forms in one hand and some pens in the other.

"Thank you for your patience, sirs," the officer said. "If you could each fill out a written statement of what you saw, you can get going. Be sure to include a good phone number and address at the top of the form. You may get contacted by a detective."

"Understood," Brunelle said as he took the form and a pen.

He stepped around the back of the patrol car and sat on the bumper to fill out his statement. He was completely sober again so the only trouble he had writing was getting the ballpoint pen to start on the damp paper.

'At approximately 2330 hours...'

But then he overheard Freddy ask the officer to step to the front of the patrol car. Curious, Brunelle strained to hear and could just make out Freddy saying, "I'm sorry, officer, but like I told you before, I'm going to decline to make any statement."

CHAPTER 9

"All rise!" commanded the bailiff as Judge LeClair entered the courtroom. "The Puyallup Tribal Court is now in session."

Brunelle rose quickly from his seat at counsel table, despite the late night. The brick in his head was an unwelcome reminder that he was well past the age when he could stay up after one o'clock and feel no worse for wear the next day. Fatigue pressed down his back. Luckily, the hotel coffee had been strong.

He had to at least pretend not to be tired. The courtroom was packed—mostly with tribal members, including at least three rows of Quilcene's extended family in the front rows. There were also two television cameras. Local stations; it was just the arraignment. But Brunelle knew the trial itself would end up being national news. Duncan had already fielded phone calls from all the major cable outlets and a half-dozen true crime shows.

"Are the parties ready in the matter of the John Quilcene?" Judge LeClair asked from his perch on the bench.

"The defense is ready," Talon announced before Brunelle could answer. He was used to replying first; that's how it was done normally. She wanted to throw him off his game.

Too bad.

"The State is ready," Brunelle announced.

Judge LeClair's face fell.

Freddy leaped to the rescue. "The *Tribe*, Your Honor. The Tribe is ready."

Shit, Brunelle thought. *And damn Talon.* He was already off his game. Not 'too bad.' Too late. He decided not to face his opponent to look at the grin he could spy out of the corner of his eye.

"Correct, Your Honor," Brunelle regained himself. "The Tribe is ready. May it please the Court, Frederick McCloud and David Brunelle on behalf of the prosecution."

He glanced down at Freddy who gave him a disapproving little shake of the head, coupled with the slightest shade of that smile of his.

"We are ready," Brunelle went on, "to proceed with the arraignment. We have filed the original criminal complaint with the clerk of the court and provided copies to defense counsel and your bailiff. It charges Mr. Quilcene with—"

"One count of murder in the first degree," the judge interrupted. "Yes, I can read, Mr. Brunelle. This is my courtroom, not yours. I shall control the proceedings."

Brunelle nodded slowly, aware of the courtroom full of eyes on his back. "Yes, Your Honor."

He knew he was going to get kicked in the crotch a lot during this trial. Better get used to it.

"Ms. Winter." The judge turned to her. "Have you had an opportunity to review the charging documents?"

"Barely, Your Honor," Talon complained. "We only received it this morning. But I've reviewed it enough to know my client is one hundred percent not guilty."

Brunelle rolled his eyes. *Why do defense attorneys always play to the cameras?*

"The plea of not guilty will be entered," LeClair declared. "Next we will discuss bail and conditions of release."

Again, Brunelle was used to going first, but he checked himself and waited for the judge to indicate whom he would hear first. It seemed to be a test; he may even have passed. After a moment, the judge smiled ever so slightly. "I'll hear first from the prosecution."

"Thank you, Your Honor," Brunelle began. "The prosecution asks the court to set bail in the amount of one million dollars. This is a charge of murder in the first degree, with a mandatory minimum sentence of twenty years in prison. He was arrested blocks away from the victim with blood on his hands. I submit to you that his responsibility for the death of George Traver is not in question. Therefore, based on his actions and the likely penalty, we believe the defendant is a flight risk and a danger to the community. One million dollars will secure his presence for future proceedings and protect the community."

Judge LeClair frowned at Brunelle for a few seconds, then turned to the other counsel table. "Ms. Winter?"

"Thank you, Your Honor." Talon stepped out from behind her large table and raised her hands slightly as she spoke. "The defense respectfully requests that Mr. Quilcene be released to the custody of his family where he can remain under house arrest, until such time as he is acquitted of the charges."

House arrest? Brunelle thought, but managed not to blurt out. *That's crazy. It's Murder One.*

He looked over at her. She had balls, so to speak; he had to give her that. Even in her perfectly tailored alpha-female suit, she had balls.

Talon gestured to the gallery. "As you can see, Your Honor, Mr. Quilcene has tremendous family support. They will act as agents of the court, ensuring that Mr. Quilcene neither flees nor poses a danger to anyone in our close-knit community."

Nice touch, Brunelle thought. The community he wasn't a part of. He hoped the judge saw through the flattery too.

"In addition," Talon's voice softened and Brunelle looked to see her pause and stiffen her chin—quite dramatic, he thought, "the court may have heard the tragic news of early this morning. Mr. Quilcene's teenage cousin—more like a little brother to my client— was brutally stabbed and murdered last night."

LeClair nodded sympathetically. "Yes, I am aware of that tragedy."

Shit, Brunelle thought again.

"Mr. Quilcene's family needs him at home, Your Honor," Talon implored. "Release him to the care of his family. You won't regret it, Your Honor."

Brunelle stopped himself from rolling his eyes. He started to stand up. "May I be heard, Your Honor?"

"No," the judge barked without taking his eyes from the defense table. "The defense request will be granted. This court believes that Mr. Quilcene poses neither a flight risk nor a danger to our close-knit community. Accordingly, home detention is appropriate and so ordered."

Quilcene's family started to squeal and clap, but Talon quieted them with a sharp shake of her head and slash of her hand.

Quilcene himself was ecstatic. Brunelle watched as his face explode into a smile and he grabbed Talon's hand to shake it emphatically.

She shakes that murderer's hand, but not mine. He surrendered a smile to himself. *Of course, I'm a jackass...*

LeClair waited a moment for the last of the family cheering to die down. "We have already scheduled our trial and pre-trial dates. Are there any other matters?"

"Yes, Your Honor," Brunelle said, standing fully this time. He reached into his file and pulled out the other pleading he had drafted before leaving the office the previous afternoon. He handed a copy to Talon and one to the bailiff to hand up to the judge.

"This is a motion," Brunelle explained, "to exclude the defendant's claim of justifiable homicide based on 'blood revenge.' We believe a careful review of the applicable law and facts will show that the defense is spurious and ought not to be argued to the jury."

LeClair pursed his lips. He looked at Talon. "Any response, counsel?"

Talon took a moment, then looked up from her initial scan of Brunelle's pleading. "Not at this time, Your Honor. I won't be ambushed into making an ill-prepared response."

Damn, Brunelle thought. That was exactly what he was hoping for.

"I would ask the court," Talon continued, "to set the matter for a hearing in two weeks. That will give me time to respond.

Brunelle looked down at Freddy and gave him a 'that's fair' shrug. Freddy offered the same back.

"And," Talon went on, with a new edge to her voice that made Brunelle look over and see her grin at him, "we can also address the defense motion to exclude."

She extracted her own pleadings from her briefcase and handed copies to Brunelle and the bailiff.

"Motion to exclude what?" Judge LeClair asked as the bailiff handed him Talon's pleading.

"To exclude Mr. Brunelle," Talon grinned. "He's not a tribal member and should not be permitted to practice before this venerable court."

CHAPTER 10

Brunelle slammed through the administration building's doors and out into the parking lot.

"Of all the racist, prejudiced, bigoted..." He shook a fist at the ground.

Freddy hurried out after him. Some of the spectators started to file out too. Luckily no cameramen yet. They stayed back to interview Talon. She was far more photogenic than Brunelle.

"Sorry about that," Freddy apologized. "She's just doing her job."

Brunelle was trying to control his anger, but he didn't feel like trying very hard. "Look," he said," I never wanted to be down in here in front of this stupid court. You people are the ones who decided to assert some archaic treaty right. You people are the ones who insisted a murder trial be held in a converted gymnasium. You people are the ones who agreed to have a real prosecutor included. And now, you people are the ones who just let a murderer out on the street because some gang thug in his family got shanked over some drug debt or fucking some rival gang member's girlfriend."

Freddy blinked at him. "You people? Dave, I'm on your

side."

Brunelle closed his eyes and sighed. "I know. That's not what I meant." He opened his eyes and put a hand on Freddy's shoulder. "I'm sorry. I know we're a team. It's just— I'm just frustrated, that's all. And tired. I'm really fucking tired."

Freddy's smile blossomed again. "No worries, partner. I'm tired too. And I don't blame you. Talon's ruthless and smart. It's actually a compliment she wants you off the case. It means she's worried about you."

A smiled cracked Brunelle's scowl. "Hm. Yeah. I hadn't thought of it that way."

"And the way she used Quilcene's cousin's murder to spring Quilcene?" Freddy shook his head admiringly. "Man, I didn't see that coming."

Brunelle could feel his heart slowing. Damn Talon for pissing him off. He wanted off the case, didn't he? Just concede the motion and drive back up to Seattle. If they wanted to walk a murderer, why should he care?

But he did care.

He looked down at Freddy. He knew he needed to do these next bits alone. Talon was a little too quick to seize onto Bobby Quilcene's murder. She was probably just a cold-hearted opportunist, but he needed more information. More information was always good. But given what he'd overheard Freddy tell the officer the previous night, Brunelle didn't think it wise to bring him along.

"I'm going to get away from here and get a few things done," Brunelle said. "Maybe you can do some more research on blood revenge? If we can convince LeClair that it didn't justify this type of murder even back when the treaty was signed, he might keep Talon from arguing it to the jury."

Freddy clicked his heels and saluted. "Yes, sir." Then he looked over at the police station. "Uh, I don't have a computer in my office yet. Maybe I'll head home to do that research."

"Perfect," Brunelle replied.

~*~

Brunelle waited for Freddy to drive away, then turned and walked into the Tribal Police station.

"Hello," he greeted the officer behind the glass—a man this time. "I was a witness to the murder last night and I'd like to speak with the detective about the case."

The officer's eyes widened just a bit. Brunelle guessed they didn't get a lot of murders in their small jurisdiction. "Yes, sir. I'll get him right now. I'm sure he'll want to talk with you."

Until he realizes who I am, Brunelle thought. "Thanks."

He took a seat in one of the three plastic chairs in the small lobby and looked down at his hands. His pale, pink hands. He was pretty sure he could make out a couple of age spots under the hair. It reminded him of the gray starting to fleck his temples. He sighed.

After a few minutes, the door buzzed and the detective stepped into the lobby. At least Brunelle assumed he was the detective. Either that or a male model. Fabio meets Geronimo. Tall, buff, chiseled features, smoldering eyes. And a gun on his hip to boot.

"Good morning, sir," he said, appraising Brunelle for a moment before extending his hand. "I'm Detective Sixrivers. Officer Jones said you were a witness to last night's homicide?"

Brunelle stood up and shook the detective's hand. "Yes. I'm Dave Brunelle. I'm a prosecutor with the King County Prosecutor's Office. I'm down here prosecuting the Quilcene case."

Sixrivers extracted his hand. "Oh. I thought Officer Jones said you were a witness."

"I was," Brunelle assured. "In fact, I was the first to the victim. But the reason I was even down here last night is that I'm prosecuting the Quilcene murder case. The defendant on that case just got released to home detention, in part because the victim last night was his cousin. I was hoping you might have time to brief me on the case."

The detective's eyebrows lowered and he crossed his arms. "I'm sorry, Mr. Brunelle. We don't discuss details of ongoing investigations. Especially with witnesses."

Brunelle frowned. "Well, I'm not just a witness. I'm a prosecutor, and that homicide is impacting my case."

"That homicide," Sixrivers said, arms still crossed, "is the subject of an ongoing investigation. I can't discuss it with you."

"Can't?" Brunelle asked. "Or won't?"

Sixrivers set his superhero-like jaw. "The bottom line is the same, Mr. Brunelle. I'm not going to discuss the case with you. If and when a suspect is identified and charged, then you may be contacted by a prosecutor. Until then, I'd suggest you forget about it."

Brunelle nodded. "Okay," he relented. "Thanks anyway, detective. I appreciate your time."

He shook Sixrivers' hand again and stepped back out into the cool autumn day. At least Sixrivers had let one thing slip.

"They don't have a suspect yet."

It wasn't much, but it was something.

His next visit should fill in at least some of the gaps.

CHAPTER 11

The Pierce County Medical Examiner's Office sat on Pacific Avenue, toward the top of a hill overlooking downtown Tacoma and Commencement Bay. When Brunelle first got the location from his GPS he thought he might be in for a nice view of the water. Instead, the ME's office was a squat, two-story building tucked, viewless, between some not quite so squat four- and five-story buildings. Its only view was across Pacific Avenue to the old brick facade of the Health Department's headquarters.

The lobby was equally unimpressive. No receptionist, no chairs. Just a metal intercom box and an elevator. Pressing the elevator call button confirmed it wouldn't light until he got the okay from whoever was on the other end of the intercom.

Brunelle pressed the intercom button. "Hello? This is Dave Brunelle from the King County Prosecutor's Office."

A few seconds later a woman's voice gave a staticky reply. "Hello. Did—*skraak*—say you're—*skrawk*—om the prosecutor's office?"

Brunelle thought for a moment. "Sure. Can I come up?"

After a moment, a loud buzzer sounded and Brunelle's

second effort at the elevator button met with success. He stepped in and pressed the only option: the basement.

Nice. The basement of the morgue. This should be cheery.

The elevator shuddered to a halt and after a few too many seconds, the doors slowly opened to reveal a very tall, very thin, very bald man glowering down at him.

"Hello," said the man. "I don't know you."

He had an accent, but Brunelle couldn't quite place it.

Brunelle smiled. "No, you don't." He put out his hand as he stepped off the elevator. "Dave Brunelle."

The man shook Brunelle's hand and cracked a disconcerting smile. "I'm Dr. Garner, the new Medical Examiner. You're with the prosecutor's office?"

"Yes, sir," Brunelle replied. He felt no compunction to clarify which county he worked for. "I'm here about last night's murder."

Garner grinned. "Which one?"

Wow, tough town. "Uh, the one by the casino?"

"Ah." Garner raised an appraising eyebrow as he led Brunelle down a narrow hallway decorated with interesting and slightly disturbing prints and multi-media displays. "Do they have someone in custody already?"

"Er..." Right, Brunelle realized. No need for a prosecutor until a defendant is identified. "No, not yet. But, uh, I'm prosecuting a related murder."

Garner nodded. "I'm not surprised to hear that. Another gang-banger, I take it. They're killing each other like crazy right now. It's the damn Hatfields and McCoys out there. The latest is Hilltop Crips and Eastside Bloods. This was our first Native Blood since I've been here. I guess the Hilltops are branching out on their retributory killings."

"Guess so," Brunelle agreed. *Or it's a different blood feud.*

"So yours is gang-related too?" Garner asked as they reached his office. He motioned Brunelle inside.

"Um, yes," Brunelle answered. "My murderer is Native Gangster Blood."

"Maybe my victim was in retribution for yours," Garner suggested.

Brunelle nodded as he sat down across from the M.E. "Yeah, that's kinda what I'm thinking too."

"So," Garner leaned back in his chair and put his hands behind his head, "what can I do for you?"

Might as well ask for the moon, Brunelle figured.

"Can I get a copy of the autopsy report?"

Garner leaned forward. "I just finished that autopsy an hour ago. Do you think I have the report done already?"

"Do you?"

"Why, yes," the medical examiner grinned. "As a matter of fact, I do. Just the rough draft, but these autopsies tend to run together. One cadaver after another. I did eight yesterday alone. I learned a long time ago to dictate each report between autopsies, not all of them at the end of the day."

He turned and patted his computer monitor. "And I just got the latest dictation software. If you don't mind the occasional wrong word—'ulterior' instead of 'anterior'—I can print you out a copy right now."

Brunelle smiled. "That would be great, doctor. Thank you so much."

"No problem at all," Garner replied.

A few mouse-clicks later the printer on his desk started to spit out the report. He collected it up and handed it to Brunelle, who stood up, took the report, and prepared to leave.

"Thanks again, doctor."

"Happy to help," Garner answered as they stepped back into the hallway. He pointed back down the strangely-decorated hallway. "The elevator will take you back up to the lobby."

"Great," said Brunelle and he headed for the exit.

"Say 'Hi' to Mark for me," Garner called out after him.

Brunelle pressed the elevator button and turned around. "Who?"

Garner looked puzzled. "Your boss?"

"Oh right," Brunelle smiled as the elevator doors opened. He stepped in. "Sure. Will do. Thanks again."

Garner's puzzled expression only deepened as the elevator doors closed glacially and Brunelle considered his next, even more uncomfortably dishonest rendezvous.

CHAPTER 12

He had to wait eight days before he could get his expert to review Dr. Garner's report. The first three because she wouldn't return his calls. The next five were because it was that long before Kat could get a baby-sitter for Lizzy. She wasn't about to leave her home alone, and Brunelle couldn't just ask her for help. He needed to take her out to dinner. Make amends for his insensitive description of Talon.

Besides, there was what he might get in exchange for dinner. A boy could dream, anyway.

He managed to wait until after the waiter had brought the entrees before starting his spiel.

"So," he tried to sound casual. "You haven't asked me how my tribal case is going."

Kat looked up, about to put a piece of beef in her mouth. She went ahead with the bite and waited to fully chew and swallow before replying sardonically, "Oh, I'm sorry, dear. How selfish of me. Please, tell me. How's your tribal case going?"

Brunelle smiled despite the sarcasm. "I'm glad you asked."

He took time for a quick bite himself. "It just expanded. Two for one, you might say."

"Really?" Kat smiled. "Did someone kill the hot bitch defense attorney?"

Brunelle managed not to reply, 'Wow' and instead said, "Uh, no. Someone killed the defendant's cousin."

"Oh," Kat said as she took another bite. She didn't even try to sound interested.

"I think they're related," Brunelle pressed on.

Kat looked at him. "Yeah, I'm pretty sure cousins are related."

"No, no," Brunelle stammered. "The cases. The cases are related."

Kat shrugged. "Okay."

"They're in the same gang. At least that's what the detective down there says."

Kat got a strange look on her face. "What's the detective's name?" she asked unexpectedly.

"Er, Sixrivers," Brunelle answered.

She nodded. "Tommy Sixrivers." It wasn't a question. More like the recounting of a pleasant memory.

"You know him too?" Brunelle asked, trying not to sound perturbed. He knew he'd failed.

"Oh, yes." Kat purred. "Dated him in high school. He was gorgeous. Only dated for a week, but oh, what a week."

"Great," Brunelle nodded. "So did you date everyone in the tribe? Like a Native American groupie or something?"

Kat's dreamy smiled twisted into a scowl. "I grew up down there. My mom is part Muckleshoot. I wasn't as cool as the Puyallup kids, but they accepted me. Some of them even thought I was attractive. Including Tommy."

"The dreamboat?" Brunelle confirmed.

The smile returned. "He's still gorgeous, isn't he?"

Brunelle sighed. "Yeah, he's pretty gorgeous."

Kat just smiled and took another bite of her dinner.

"Can we talk about the case again?" Brunelle complained.

"Sure," Kat said through her food. She swallowed. "Go ahead. Do I have to listen?"

"Ha ha," Brunelle replied. "I guess I'll just sit here knowing all about how the wounds are really similar to Traver's and not say a thing about your area of expertise."

Kat raised an eyebrow but didn't say anything.

"Yep. Pretty similar," Brunelle continued, suppressing a grin. "I mean, what do I know? I'm just a lawyer. But, you're not listening anyway, so, you know, never mind."

He took a sip of wine. He wanted her truly invested. He was going to make her ask.

So she did.

"Fine. How are the wounds similar?"

Gotcha. Brunelle let the smile push through. By the time he was done, she might even think she was the one who'd asked him out.

"Stab wounds," he said. "One to the gut, one to the heart. Except..."

"Except what?"

"Except the cousin also had one to the back. Hit his kidney."

Kat set down her fork. "And how do you know that?"

"Two reasons, actually," Brunelle answered. "First, I was a witness—"

"You saw him get stabbed?" Kat interrupted.

Brunelle shook his head. "No, I didn't actually see it. I heard him scream and ran over to him, but it was too late. He was dead on the spot. I guess a knife in your heart will do that."

Kat offered a pained smile. "And what do you know about knives in your heart, Mr. Brunelle?"

For the first time in probably too long, Brunelle didn't know what to say. Any witty remark got stuck in his throat as he looked into the soft eyes across the table from him. Before he could regain himself or figure out what to say, Kat looked down at her plate again.

"So was this one in Pioneer Square too?" she asked. "I don't remember hearing about it from the other M.E.s."

"No," Brunelle answered, relieved not to have to talk about Kat's heart after all. "It was in Pierce County. In the parking lot of that casino by I-5."

Kat looked up again. "What were you doing at the casino? You don't seem like a gambler, Mr. Brunelle."

"Of course I'm a gambler," Brunelle grinned. "I'm a trial lawyer. Every case is like the ultimate gamble."

Kat shook her head. "Do you tell the victim's family that before opening statement?"

"I usually avoid saying anything like that at any time," Brunelle replied. "Besides, it's not really gambling if you know you're going to win."

"Nice," Kat grimaced. "Callous and cocky. Great combination."

"It's endearing after a while," Brunelle assured. "I promise."

Kat wagged her finger at him. "No, no. Don't start promising things. Nothing good ever comes from a man promising things to a woman."

Brunelle stopped for a moment to consider her assertion. She took advantage of the silence to steer the conversation back on track.

"So anyway," she said. "Why were you in a Pierce County casino parking lot not quite witnessing a murder?"

"It was the night before the arraignment," Brunelle explained. "I spent the night at a hotel down there so I wouldn't be late the next morning. I was walking across the parking lot on my way back to the hotel when I heard the kid scream."

"Kid?"

"Yeah," Brunelle frowned. "Turns out he was sixteen."

"Ouch. That's not much older than Lizzy."

"Yeah, but Lizzy's not a gang member with a cousin up for murder."

Kat nodded. "Thank God for that. So, cousins, huh? And both gang-bangers. But thirty miles apart. Probably not related, Sherlock. You might want to leave the sleuthing to the detectives."

Brunelle nodded casually. "That's what I was thinking too," he said looking down at his plate and pushing some food around absently, "until I compared their autopsy report with yours."

Kat took a sip of her wine. "Are the wounds really that similar?"

Brunelle grinned and pulled out his cell phone. "See for yourself. I scanned the reports and emailed them to my phone."

Kat took the phone and began tapping the screen. Brunelle ate silently as she read the reports, muttering medical examiner phrases like 'sharp force trauma' and 'peritoneal membrane.'

"David." She finally looked up. "These injuries are basically identical."

Brunelle nodded. "I know," he said through a mouthful of salmon.

"Even the length of the incision and the depth of the wound," Kat remarked. "I mean, if I didn't know better, I'd say it was the same knife."

"Thank you, doctor," Brunelle replied with a smile. "No further questions."

Kat jerked her face from the phone screen. "No further questions? What? You knew I'd say that?"

"I hoped you would," Brunelle shrugged. "I thought the same thing, but you're the expert, not me, so you need to say it."

"Is that what this was all about?" Kat threw down her fork. "This whole fucking dinner? Just to cross examine me?"

Brunelle could feel his face starting to flush. "Well, to begin with, it's direct examination. You're my witness."

"Like hell I am, David Brunelle," Kat spat. "I'm not your anything."

The other diners were starting to look over. "Look. I'm sorry," Brunelle whispered. "It's just shop talk. I, I thought you'd be interested."

"Bullshit," Kat sneered. "You knew I wasn't returning your calls. You were afraid I was mad at you. So you finally asked me out to dinner again. You figured I wouldn't help you if I was mad at you, so you had to give in and ask me out again."

Brunelle shook his head, but kept his eyes cast downward. "No. That's not it."

Kat scoffed. "Of course it is, Mr. Callous-and-Cocky. And I finally saw through it. But not until you got what you wanted. You bastard."

The waiter hurried over to their table. "Are you ready for the check?" he suggested nervously.

"Oh, no," Kat replied with a glare at Brunelle. "Bring me a dessert menu, my good man. My date's paying so I'm going all out tonight."

"Very good," the waiter answered. He turned to Brunelle. "Would you also like a dessert menu, sir?"

"No, thanks," Brunelle squeaked. "I'm not getting any tonight.

Kat laughed darkly. "You got that right, buddy."

CHAPTER 13

The only saving grace to the crash-and-burn that was dinner with Kat was the fact that it pissed Brunelle off to be called out like that. And since there was no chance he'd be distracted with further dates in the foreseeable future, he was able to channel his anger into the work of preparing for the motions hearing in front of Judge LeClair.

Moreover, since one of the two motions was to disqualify him from the case and he was getting pretty tired of being the paleface, outsider, punching bag, he didn't spend too much time on that one. In fact, he may have spent more time trying to convince Duncan to let him concede the motion than actually writing the response, which consisted of little more than pointing out that his presence on the case had been a carefully negotiated agreement between two sovereigns in the exercise of a tenuous and politically charged treaty.

That left Brunelle plenty of time to prepare for his argument regarding Talon's bullshit 'blood revenge' defense. His initial motion to suppress was a simple two page document, but it was followed by a twenty-plus page, heavily footnoted brief explaining why the defense was, historically and legally speaking, a load of crap. It was little more than a thinly veiled attempt at jury nullification—an effort to wink at the jury, tell them the victim basically deserved it, and hope they let the murderer walk despite the law.

Brunelle was a trial lawyer. His skills lay in the courtroom, not the law library. Giving opening statements, cross examining witnesses, bringing the house down with monumental closing arguments. Writing briefs was not his strong suit. He'd hated his stint in the drug unit, responding to all those motions to suppress for allegedly illegal searches, and he'd managed to avoid the appellate unit altogether. He'd have been happy never to write another brief in his life. But this brief—'Prosecutor's Memorandum of Law in Support of Motion to Exclude Proffered Defense'—was pretty damn good, if he did say so himself.

It hit just the right balance between respect for tribal tradition and due deference to insistence on justice. He delved into their own history to show why—even within their own culture—that defense shouldn't be available to Quilcene. It was one thing for Brunelle to say, 'Our law doesn't allow this.' But it was quite another to be able to say, 'And neither does *yours*.'

He was proud to have written it.

He just wished he hadn't let Freddy argue it. "Great brief," Freddy had said the week before when they met to prepare for the hearing. This time, Freddy had driven up to Seattle—he'd insisted on it. 'Always looking for an excuse to come up to the big city,' he'd said, followed quickly by, 'Oh, and can you get me free parking? It was murder last time I went up there.'

"But," Freddy had flashed that grin of his, "you should let me argue it."

"Why?" Brunelle had felt a bit possessive of his hard work.

"Well, to be honest," Freddy shrugged, "because you're white and I'm Native. Your whole point is that our tribal law wouldn't support the defense. Judge LeClair isn't going to like an outsider telling him what his law is. He's likely to rule against you just to prove a point. But let me argue it and that aspect goes away. Just three tribal members discussing the application of tribal law. And no bossy White Man trying to tell us what to do."

It had made sense, so Brunelle had agreed. And it might have worked too, if Freddy had actually argued Brunelle's brief. But he didn't. Brunelle could only sit at counsel table and cringe as Freddy veered quickly from reasoned analysis to emotional diatribe.

"May it please the court," Freddy started innocuously enough. "I have the honor of arguing the prosecution's motion to exclude Ms. Winter's proffered defense of blood revenge. Has the court had an opportunity to read our brief?"

Everyone seemed surprised that Freddy was going to argue the motion. Brunelle had authored the written memorandum, so it would have been usual for him to present the oral argument as well. Not to mention the fact that Brunelle was the seasoned prosecutor and Freddy was... well, Brunelle hadn't quite figured that out yet, but Freddy was definitely not seasoned. And he was about to prove it.

Talon seemed especially irritated. She had been clear that she wanted to kick Brunelle's ass, not Freddy's.

Judge LeClair seemed intrigued. "Yes, I've read Mr., Brunelle's brief."

"Good," Freddy replied with a dismissive wave of his hand. "Then I won't waste any time repeating his arguments."

Brunelle slowly raised his gaze from his notepad to his co-counsel. *Uh oh.*

"Instead," Freddy almost yelled, "I want this court to consider allowing Ms. Winter's defense. And then some!"

Brunelle's eyes widened. "What are you doing?" he whispered brusquely, but Freddy ignored him.

"Yes!" Freddy threw up his arms. "By all means, let's embrace our noble and savage past, and declare open season on all who prey on the innocent. Child molesters and elder abusers beware: your lives are worthless in the eyes of the Great Spirit."

Oh, fuck. Brunelle lowered his head into his hands. He hoped the judge might stop Freddy, but no such luck.

Freddy extended calming hands to everyone in the courtroom. "I know, I know. I'm exaggerating. For effect. But this is a serious issue—one that deserves serious consideration. What the defense is arguing is that, because the tribal jurisdiction for this trial rests in an ancient treaty, then we should apply ancient tribal law. That is, the law and custom of our tribe at the time of the ratification of the treaty. Well, fine, then. Let's do that."

Brunelle looked up again. He had to admit, he was curious where Freddy was headed with it all. A glance around the courtroom confirmed that the judge and gallery were engaged. Even Talon had set down her pen and was watching Freddy intently, her pretty face resting on her manicured fist.

"Let's ignore," Freddy continued, "some of those ancient Native traditions revolving around things like slavery and women's rights. Let's ignore the fact that every culture matures and progresses and abandons practices it later comes to find outdated or even abhorrent. Let's assume nothing ever changes and what was once a crime or defense is always a crime or defense.

"Ms. Winter wants the court to instruct the jury that they should acquit the defendant if they find that he killed the victim in retaliation for the molestations of his niece by that same victim. Fine, let's do it."

"Freddy…" Brunelle whispered, but to no avail.

"But let's also instruct them," Freddy proposed, "that someone from Mr. Quilcene's family must be killed to settle the debt created by the murder of George Traver."

Gasps thrilled through the gallery. Talon just stared at him over her blood-red fingernails. Brunelle rubbed the bridge of his nose. He wondered just how far Freddy would go with it.

"Let's get photographs of every member of Quilcene's family," Freddy suggested. "Grandmas and babies and fourth cousins thrice removed. Let's write some bios for the jury. Let's really let them know who's who in the defendant's family. Maybe even a PowerPoint presentation, complete with soundtrack and the sounds of children playing and laughing."

He paused.

"And then we make the jury pick which one of them dies. Which one dies to settle the score with the defendant? He upped the ante when he killed George Traver. Traver is dead, Now, someone in Quilcene's family must die."

Talon finally reacted. "Objection, Your Honor. Counsel is completely mischaracterizing my argument."

"Objection overruled," Judge LeClair said without even looking at her. "Continue, Mr. McCloud."

"Thank you, Your Honor," Freddy nodded to the judge. "Yes, by all means. Let's get more blood. This is blood revenge after all, correct? Blood revenge leads to blood feuds, and we all know feuds never really end. They're feuds. That's the whole point. They never stop. Hell, this one has just started. One death isn't a blood feud. It's murder. But two deaths? Three? More? Now we're talking."

Brunelle found himself staring at Freddy, transfixed by the audacity of his argument.

"So, the only question is: who is worth the life of George

Traver, the child molester? There probably aren't that many people that low. Our next victim would need to be a criminal himself. Someone immersed in the criminal lifestyle. Someone who holds himself out as a thug. Someone who, if he ended up with the same damn knife in his own chest, no one would miss any more than George Traver."

Brunelle's eyes widened. 'The same knife.' *Oh my God.*

"But will that end it?" Freddy asked rhetorically. "Not likely. It's a feud, remember? A blood feud. Our glorious tradition of blood revenge often led to another one of our glorious traditions: the Mourning War, where the revenge never stopped and families and tribes were trapped in a never-ending cycle of revenge and murder. So I say, if we're going to let the jury have this question—if they're going to be asked to apply ancient tribal custom as modern day law—then let's really make them do it. If they say 'not guilty' by reason of blood revenge, then they have to fill out a blood feud schedule. Five or six members of each family and the order in which they should be killed."

Brunelle looked over at the defense table. Talon was just shaking her head, waiting her turn. Quilcene was staring daggers at Freddy.

Fitting, Brunelle thought.

"That leaves one question to resolve," Freddy declared. "Who will carry out the killings? The jury? the judge? Maybe our tribal police? Or best yet, just leave it to the members of our community to kill each other, according to our custom. As long as they stick to the schedule, they won't be held any more accountable for their murderous acts than Johnny Quilcene was for the premeditated intentional murder of George Traver."

The courtroom reverberated in stunned silence for several seconds.

Finally, Judge LeClair asked, "Are you done?"

Freddy, who was practically panting after his impassioned monologue, took a couple more deep breaths and nodded. "yes, Your Honor. Thank you."

LeClair nodded back, his expression inscrutable. He turned to Talon. "Response?"

Talon stood up and threw her silky hair over her shoulder. "Thank you, Your Honor. To begin with, I'm not even sure which argument to respond to: Mr. Brunelle's specious treatise on our legal traditions, or Mr. McCloud's ridiculous melodrama." She smoothed out her suit. "I suppose I'll start with Mr. Brunelle's written brief…"

Freddy sat down next to Brunelle, still breathing heavily, and stared straight ahead. Talon was launching into her attack on Brunelle's perfectly crafted brief, but he didn't bother listening. He'd been around long enough to know that LeClair was going to rule however he was going to rule. One of the biggest delusions trial attorneys nursed was the belief that they ever really influenced the judge. LeClair had probably made up his mind about Talon's defense the same morning she first proposed it at the status conference, anticipating and weighing every argument in advance.

Well, almost every argument.

"Impressive," Brunelle whispered to Freddy as Talon droned on. "Did you rehearse that or was it all impromptu?"

Freddy looked down and shook his head. His grin peeked out of the corner of his mouth. "A little of both, actually."

Brunelle nodded. "You were smart not to tell me what you were going to say. There's no way I would have let you argue that if I'd known."

The grin widened. "Yeah, I kind of figured that."

"But actually," Brunelle went on. "That's not what I found really impressive."

Freddy turned and looked askance.

"What's really impressive," Brunelle observed with his own subdued grin, "is that hidden in that overly dramatic, hyperbolic, even buffoonish diatribe, was the fact that you actually believe it."

Freddy affected a laugh. "Naw. I was just exaggerating. Trying to make a point."

Brunelle shook his head. "You're not fooling me. That was too passionate. You'd be just fine to let the families fight this out and leave the cops and the courts out of it."

Freddy stared at Brunelle for several second, then down at the table. "Yeah, well, that's not really an option, so it doesn't really matter."

Brunelle took a moment to look up at Talon. She was still talking. It seemed like she had moved on to part II, Freddy's argument. Based on where she seemed to be in her presentation, Brunelle figured she'd talk for another three, maybe five minutes.

"I would think," Brunelle whispered as he turned back to face Freddy, "that the bigger problem is Traver doesn't have any surviving family."

Freddy turned away again. "Is that right?" he whispered.

"Yeah. I'm pretty sure I told you that at the casino the other night."

Freddy didn't reply.

"What would happen then, Freddy?" Brunelle pressed. "What happened to the blood feud if one side ran out of family members? Would that end it?"

Freddy shrugged. "It could."

"But it might not?" Brunelle asked.

"Depends."

"On what?"

Freddy shifted in his seat. "On whether another member of

the tribe agreed to take up the feud on behalf of the victim."

Brunelle frowned and ran a hand through his hair. "That's what I was afraid you were going to say."

"...and for those reasons," Talon was summing up, "the court should deny the prosecution's motion to exclude the defense of justifiable homicide by way of blood revenge. Thank you."

Talon sat down and gave Brunelle a 'How ya like them apples?' smirk. He almost wished he'd listened to her.

"Any rebuttal, Mr. Brunelle?" the judge asked with a raised eyebrow. The direction of his question to Brunelle and not Freddy was clearly intentional. Also clear, from the expression on his face, was the fact that he really didn't want to listen to any more lawyers talking.

"No, Your Honor," Brunelle replied. "Thank you."

Silence fell over the courtroom as Judge LeClair nodded and raised pressed fingertips to his lips. "This is a difficult question," he began. "One with wide-ranging impact. There is no doubt that current Washington law would not permit a jury to consider this killing to be justifiable homicide. At least not for the reasons put forward by Ms. Winter. Under Washington law, this would be a vigilante killing at best, cold-blooded revenge at worst. Under Washington law, this would be murder."

He paused to take a sip of water.

"But this isn't a Washington court. This is the Puyallup Indian Tribal Court. And this court's jurisdiction arises pursuant to a treaty between the Tribe and the government of the United States. And that treaty is over one hundred years old. So the threshold question is: Does this court apply Washington law of today, or tribal law of last century?"

Brunelle looked at Freddy again. He knew they disagreed on the answer to that question.

"If I decide that Washington law applies," Judge LeClair continued, "then that ends the inquiry and the defense is excluded. But if I decided that tribal law applies, then there is a secondary question: would this really have been a defense?"

Brunelle nodded. He was right. LeClair had already analyzed this upside down and sideways. Maybe Freddy didn't do any damage after all.

"Ms. Winter asserts that it would have been a defense," LeClair observed. "And interestingly, Mr. McCloud agrees."

Then again... Brunelle glowered at Freddy.

"Accordingly, who am I to disagree? The prosecution motion to exclude the defense of blood revenge is denied."

A ripple of murmured cheers filtered through Quilcene's friends and family in the gallery.

"Yesss," Talon hissed under her breath. She turned and looked at Brunelle. "Your ass," she whispered. "Kicked. By me."

Brunelle rolled his eyes. He was really starting to dislike her. And it really pissed him off that she was so hot. He tried not to think about what he wanted to do to her ass.

"The next motion," Judge LeClair announced, "is the defendant's motion to disqualify Mr. Brunelle from the prosecution of this case."

"Your Honor?" Talon jumped to her feet. "The defense would ask the court to delay the hearing on that motion."

"Delay?" Brunelle and the judge asked at the same time.

"For how long?" Judge LeClair demanded suspiciously.

"And why?" Brunelle added.

"Just a few minutes," Talon answered. "And because I need to speak with Mr. Brunelle. In private."

CHAPTER 14

Talon closed the conference room door behind her and turned to face Brunelle. Her hands were behind her, still on the doorknob, and her hair cascaded around her face, which was tipped forward, eyes inviting and dangerous. He could smell her perfume. Jasmine. They were alone.

Enemy, Brunelle told himself over the blood rushing in his ears. *Remember, she's the enemy.*

"David," she started. Not Brunelle. Not Jackass. Not even a simple 'Dave.' *David.* She was good. "Let's talk."

Brunelle swallowed. He wasn't even sure he could talk. "Okay," he croaked. "What do you want to talk about?"

"Us," she said, finally releasing the doorknob and taking a step toward him. Her hips swung as she walked. "And this case."

Us? What the fuck does that mean? "Okay. Talk."

Talon's mouth spread into a full-lipped smile. She crossed her arms, which only succeeded in pulling her well-tailored jacket even tighter against her frame. "Did you see how I kicked your ass just now?"

"Actually," Brunelle raised a finger, "you kicked Freddy's

ass."

The smile twisted into a grimace. "Yeah, I know. That was no fun at all. I already know I can kick his ass. It's your ass I want."

Oh, Talon, Brunelle managed not to say. *I want yours too.*

"Sorry about that," he said instead. "I didn't know he was going to argue that. I wouldn't have let him if I'd known."

"Well, still," Talon pressed on, another step into his comfort zone. "You have to admit, my argument against your written brief was pretty amazing."

Brunelle shrugged. "I'm sure it was. I wasn't really listening."

Talon's perfectly shaped shoulders fell.

"I was busy," Brunelle explained, "yelling at Freddy. In whispers, of course, but it distracted me from your undoubtedly stunning oral skills."

Brunelle winced. *Nice choice of words, counselor.*

Talon shook her head, apparently oblivious to his phraseology. "That damn Freddy. He's already screwing things up."

"To your advantage," Brunelle noted.

"Whatever. There's no challenge. No glory in taking him down. He doesn't even have a real job."

Brunelle bristled at that. "Prosecutor is a real job, even a smaller assignment like tribal prosecutor."

Talon cocked her head at Brunelle. Her eyes held back a laugh. "He's not the tribal prosecutor, Dave. There is no tribal prosecutor."

Brunelle offered a puzzled expression. "But I thought…"

"This court doesn't normally handle criminal matters," Talon explained. "That's why this is such a big deal. Usually it's just family and child welfare matters. And parking tickets. Lots of parking tickets. Pays for the casino."

"I thought the casino paid for the casino," Brunelle

remarked, recalling the fifty dollars he'd dropped the other night.

Talon laughed lightly. A perfect little laugh. "Yeah, I suppose it does. Fine, the parking tickets pay the judge's salary. But they don't pay for a prosecutor too."

Brunelle thought for a moment. "So where does Freddy normally work then? Pierce County Prosecutor's Office? Tacoma City Attorney?"

Talon shook her head and let out another perfectly dark little laugh. "No, he doesn't have a law job at all. He couldn't find one after law school. He had given up and was working as a bank teller or something. But when the tribe decided to do this, they wanted tribal members as the lawyers. Freddy's a member and he's got a bar card, so *voilà*, he's the prosecutor."

Brunelle pointed at her. "So you're not the public defender?"

"Oh, please!" Talon scowled. "Don't offend me."

"It's not an insult," Brunelle replied instantly. "The best defense attorneys I go against are public defenders. Dedicated to the cause, not the fee."

Talon took a moment to consider. "So, you're complimenting me?"

Fuck. Brunelle fought off a juvenile blush. "I suppose I am," he admitted. Then he pushed the conversation along. "So where do you work usually? Or don't you have a law job either?"

"Oh, no, I have a law job," Talon nodded confidently. "I'm a senior litigation associate at Gordon, High and Steinmetz. I'm one experienced-homicide-prosecutor-ass-kicking away from making partner."

Brunelle grimaced at the corporate ritual of 'making partner.' The reward for seven years of slavish, round the clock-and-calendar work for the already rich partners. "Well, congratulations," he managed to say.

Talon frowned at him. "Don't judge me, Mr. Public Servant. It's a good job and I'm damn good at it. The tribe called me first. I could have chosen to be the prosecutor, but I chose defense."

Brunelle's eyebrows shot up. "Why?"

Talon laughed again. "Well, the first reason is, I'd rather defend the guy who killed the child molester than try to vindicate the child molester."

"I'm not trying to vindicate anyone." Brunelle put his hands up. "I'm just trying to enforce the law. Murder is murder."

"Unless it's justified," Talon teased.

Brunelle just shook his head. "What's the second reason?"

Talon's eyes sparkled. "When they told me a senior prosecutor was coming down from Seattle to prosecute the case, I knew I'd much rather notch my belt with a victory over him than carry his briefcase."

Brunelle had to nod. It made sense. "You're going to use me to make a name for yourself, huh?"

"My phone isn't going to stop ringing once word gets out that I got an acquittal for a guilty-as-hell murder defendant."

"You're that sure you're going to win?"

Talon offered a delicious grin. "Yep. And you know it too."

Brunelle pursed his lips. He didn't know it, but he didn't mind her being overconfident either.

"Unless..." Talon started.

Brunelle narrowed his eye suspiciously. "Unless what?"

"Unless you offer my guy a manslaughter. Then we both win and go back to our real jobs."

"Manslaughter?" Brunelle was incredulous. "He stabbed him in the heart. That's murder."

"Naw," Talon waved it away. "Murder is intentional. That was reckless. An accident."

Brunelle thought for a moment. "The heart," he repeated. "He stabbed him directly in the heart."

"Lucky shot," Talon insisted. "No one studies anatomy any more."

Brunelle looked down at the left side of his own chest. "Everyone knows where the heart is."

"Lucky shot," Talon repeated. "Manslaughter One. Then we go our separate ways."

Brunelle suddenly realized he was in no hurry to go separate ways from Talon, but that wasn't the point, or his motivation. "I'm not giving you a manslaughter."

"Fine," Talon shrugged. "I'll get it from the jury then, if they don't just acquit outright. There's no way they convict my guy, especially after the ruling I just got. It means I get to bring in all the sick shit your guy ever did."

"Traver is not *my* guy," Brunelle insisted. "My guy is Lady Justice. Well, my gal. Whatever. Anyway, the only stuff that will come in is what your guy knew at the time of the murder. Which means you have to put him on the stand. Which means I get to cross examine his ass."

Talon laughed. "You think so, huh? Nope, Judge LeClair is going to let me bring in every last sick-fuck thing Traver ever did to anybody. And you know it too. Have you even talked with the mom of your guy's last victim? Johnny's sister? Have you seen her daughter? Do you know how much the jury is going to love my guy after I put that little princess on the stand and she tells them what that bastard did to her?"

Brunelle paused. He knew she was right. The judge was going to let it all in. *Damn it.*

"I told you," Talon said. "I'm going to kick your ass. And get rich from doing it. And you're going to lose a slam-dunk, blood-on-his hands case and crawl back to Seattle with your tail between your legs."

Brunelle rubbed his chin. "Talon?" he said.

"Yes, David?" He voice was like a chainsaw purring.

"You're overconfident." He crossed his arms and smiled. "Get ready to get schooled."

Talon returned the grin with a broad smile, her full lips parting to show off her perfect teeth. "Let the battle begin."

~*~

"Talon and Brunelle returned to the courtroom and the bailiff went to fetch the judge.

"What happened in there?" Freddy asked Brunelle when he got to their table.

"I'll tell you later," Brunelle replied. "We've got some work to do."

"All rise!" the bailiff commanded as Judge LeClair retook the bench.

"Are you ready to argue your motion, Ms. Winter?"

Talon stayed standing as Brunelle and Freddy sat down. "The defense withdraws its motion to disqualify Mr. Brunelle. Indeed, we welcome his presence on the case. We believe it will enrich all of us."

The judge nodded slowly, then turned to the prosecution table. "Any comment, Mr. Brunelle?"

"None, Your Honor," Brunelle replied.

LeClair nodded. "Then the motion is withdrawn, and Mr. Brunelle shall remain on the case. Anything further at this time?"

"No, Your Honor," Talon answered first.

"No, Your Honor," Brunelle agreed.

Then LeClair adjourned court and left the bench. Freddy turned to Brunelle and put a hand on his shoulder. "Sorry."

"Sure," Brunelle replied. "We can talk about your argument in a minute."

"No, not that." Freddy shook his head. He pointed at Talon. "*That*. She really is going to kick your ass."

Brunelle looked at Talon and frowned as he considered how the trial would likely unfold.

"Yeah," he sighed. "I know."

CHAPTER 15

Brunelle wanted to talk to Freddy right away. They had a lot to discuss—and not just case prep. Brunelle had several very specific questions for Freddy about his very specific blood feud argument.

But Freddy begged off. He insisted he didn't have time just then. 'Personal matters' and 'previously scheduled appointments' took priority. Brunelle decided not to argue. There would be time later. And the next bit would be sensitive. Probably better to do it alone anyway. Or at least without Freddy cheerleading for a Mourning War.

Quilcene's sister's name was Stacy. The niece was Caitlyn. Three years old. *Nice.* They lived in a single-wide on the back half of the reservation. Brunelle parked his Ford Jackass on the curbless road in front of the house and walked through the toys strewn across the walkway to the front door. Putting on his best 'sympathetic professional' mask, he knocked on the screen door.

The sound of children playing leaked through the windows. After a moment, the interior door flew open and a heavy-set Native woman was staring at Brunelle through the screen.

"Hello, ma'am. My name is Dave Brunelle. I'm from the King County Prosecutor's Office. I was wondering if you had a few minutes to chat?"

Stacy Quilcene's eyes narrowed. "Prosecutor? You the one prosecuting Johnny?"

Brunelle shrugged and tried to smile lightly. "I'm afraid so. Do you have a moment to talk about his case?"

"I ain't talking to no prosecutor," Stacy said and started to close the door.

"Talon Winter said I should talk to you."

The door stopped. "Johnny's lawyer?" Stacy asked. Brunelle knew Talon would already have met with her. Always three steps ahead.

"Yes, Johnny's lawyer."

Stacy set her jaw. "Johnny's lawyer said I should talk to you?"

"That's not exactly what she said," Brunelle replied, always the lawyer. "She said *I* should talk to *you*. She was trying to convince me to cut Johnny a deal. She said I should talk to you about what happened to your daughter."

That was all accurate, Brunelle knew. He also knew he'd left out the most important part: that he told Talon no deals. He wasn't there to be convinced Johnny Quilcene deserved a manslaughter. He was there to discover what Stacy was going to tell the jury. So he could prepare to neutralize it.

Stacy chewed her lip for a few seconds, then punched the handle to the door and turned around. "Okay, come on in." She walked back into the house. "Gimme a second while I put in a video. I kinda run a daycare here for the neighbors."

Brunelle walked in and assessed the home. He didn't bother looking for her daycare license. Toys and half-empty plates littered the place. A TV in the front room was muted and tuned to some daytime drama-talk show. He heard the kids from the back bedroom, arguing over which video they were going to watch. There were two camps: Dora and Pokémon—with a lone dissenter simply sobbing.

Sometimes he regretted never having gotten married and had kids. This was a nice reminder not to regret.

He heard the video start—Dora had triumphed—and Stacy returned to collapse into the couch by the window. Brunelle sat in one of the small armchairs on the other side of the small room.

"Okay," Stacy exhaled, clearly relishing the chance to sit down for a moment. "What do you want to talk about?"

Brunelle frowned and looked down, rubbing his hands slightly. He needed to affect the right balance of empathy and professionalism.

"Tell me what happened to your daughter."

Brunelle raised his face again. Stacy's face fought to control its expression.

"Yeah, I figured that was it," she said. "Why don't you say it the right way?"

Brunelle cocked his head. "The right way?"

"Nothing *happened* to my daughter," Stacy declared. "the weather *happens*. Car crashes *happen*. Hurricanes and earthquakes and fire drills—those just happen. Ask me what George Traver *did* to my daughter."

Brunelle nodded. She was absolutely right. "Okay. What did George Traver do to your daughter?"

Stacy looked down the hallway at the Dora screening. She turned back and met Brunelle's eyes fiercely. "You mean besides destroying her innocence? Besides teaching her never to trust anyone ever again? Teaching her to blame herself for other people's sick actions? For thinking she's dirty and worthless and broken? Being afraid of every man in her life? Johnny? Her own fucking dad? You mean besides that?"

Brunelle swallowed. He was used to victims unleashing their anger in his presence, but that was when he was on their side. They were sharing, coping, purging—not raging at him.

He nodded again, slowly, his hands pressed into a twisted knot. "No," he said softly. "Never mind. I don't need to know any more than that."

And in a way, he didn't. He didn't need to drive home thinking about the details of George Traver's fat sweaty body and the owner of one of those giggles down the hall. What mattered was how Stacy would present to the jury. And she'd present great—for Talon. *Damn it.*

"The only thing I really need to know is whether Johnny knew. Did Johnny know what happened to, uh…?"

He'd forgotten the girl's name already. *Damn it again.*

"Caitlyn," Stacy reminded him. "And yes. of course he did. Everyone did. You don't hide that sort of thing. It just makes it worse."

Brunelle nodded. "How did Johnny react when he found out? Were you there?"

"I was the one who told him," Stacy sneered. "How did he react?" She laughed and shook her head. "He went fucking nuts. He's NGB. Did you know that?"

"Yeah," Brunelle answered. "He's got it tattooed across his chest. Kinda hard to miss."

"Yeah, well, you don't fuck with NGB."

Now that phrase might help him in front of the jury. Noble uncle seeking justice, or just violent gang thug?

"Did Johnny usually carry a weapon," he asked.

"No." Stacy shook her head.

No, of course not, Brunelle thought sarcastically. *What gang member carries a weapon?*

"We have the knife," Brunelle explained. "Did he carry that knife often?"

"That knife?" Stacy repeated. "No, that knife was special."

"Special?"

"Have you seen it?" Stacy asked.

"Not since the night of the murder," Brunelle admitted. "And I was a bit distracted."

He realized he had another errand to run. He stood up to take his leave.

Stacy stood up too and they made their way to the front door.

"So," she asked, "are you gonna give Johnny the deal?"

Brunelle looked down. He shoved one hand into his pocket and set his other on the doorknob. Without turning to face her, he opened the door and shook his head. "No."

CHAPTER 16

Brunelle tried to shake the memory of children giggling and yelling '¡*Vamanos!*' as he turned the corner and clacked down the long concrete hallway in the basement of Seattle P.D.'s main precinct.

Chen was waiting for him in front of the property room.

"You're late," Chen said in greeting, giving his watch an exaggerated glance.

"Nice to see you too," Brunelle replied. "Thanks for always being happy to make time for me."

Chen laughed. "Just giving you a hard time. Although I would like to make this quick. I've got a million and one things on my desk."

"I know the feeling," Brunelle commiserated as he reached the detective. "It'll be quick. There's just one thing I want to look at, but I definitely don't want to do it alone. Always have a witness when you look at evidence. Prosecutor 101."

Chen nodded. "Understood. I'm just glad I didn't have to drive down to the tribal police station. I was afraid they would have moved the evidence down there too."

Brunelle shook his head. "I don't think they even have an evidence room. They barely have a courtroom."

Chen laughed again. "Great. Looking forward to testifying down there. If I can find it."

Brunelle actually felt a little bad. He was starting to respect LeClair at least. "Okay, well, let's get this done. I just want to see the knife."

Chen knocked on the window and an evidence officer promptly appeared.

"Item number one on this case, please." Chen slid the young officer a copy of the first property sheet on the case and pointed to the case number.

The officer gave a, "Be right back," and disappeared with Chen's paperwork.

"So," Chen turned to Brunelle, "how's it going so far?"

Brunelle rolled his eyes. "Great. My victim was a scumbag who deserved to die."

"I told you that already," Chen reminded him.

"Yes, you did. And now the judge is going to let the defense attorney tell the jury. So that'll be two of you."

"Three," Chen corrected. "Don't forget Kat."

"Not likely," Brunelle let slip. "So, yeah, three of you."

Before Chen could press him on Kat, the officer returned. "Uh, detective? You wanted to see the knife, right?"

"Right," Chen answered, concern tingeing the word.

"Er, I'm afraid there's a problem."

"A problem?" Brunelle inserted himself. His pulse quickened. "It's the fucking murder weapon. There better not be any problems."

The evidence officer slid Chen's copy of the property sheets back to the detective, then pushed the property room's originals under the glass. He pointed to a stamp on the originals marked 'Evidence Viewing.' "We use this stamp whenever someone checks out evidence. It has blank lines to fill in the date and time, and also for the viewer to sign the item out of evidence and back in again. But there's only one signature here."

The evidence officer looked up at them. "It looks like the knife got pulled for a viewing, but then never returned."

Chen snatched up the paperwork as Brunelle's stomach flipped. "Who checked it out?" the detective demanded even as he scanned the page.

The officer shook his head. "I don't recognize the name."

Chen looked up from the sheets. "Who the hell is 'F. McCloud'?"

Brunelle couldn't believe it. Or worse yet, he could.

"Freddy."

CHAPTER 17

5:00. Freddy's 'office' in the Tribal Police H.Q.

That's where they agreed to meet. It was a long drive from Seattle in afternoon traffic and Freddy had claimed 'stuff' to do, but Brunelle had insisted on the meeting. And on neutral—and safe—ground.

Brunelle got there early and checked in with Sixrivers in his back corner office. He didn't tell him everything he had planned—there was a chance Freddy could explain it without law enforcement having to be called in—but Brunelle figured he should explain his presence in the precinct.

"Just meeting with Freddy," he assured.

Sixrivers slid aside whatever file he was looking at. "Can I give you some advice?"

Brunelle shrugged. "Sure."

"Go home."

Brunelle was surprised. "Go home? What does that mean?"

"It means," Sixrivers leaned back and crossed his arms, "you should go back to Seattle and forget all about this little case."

"I would if I could," Brunelle admitted. "You think I want to be down here, in some unfamiliar court, before a judge I don't know, applying century-old law, against a defense attorney who wants to skin me alive? Believe me, I've tried, but my boss won't let me off the case. I'm stuck down here."

Sixrivers nodded. "Too bad. But I understand. I've got superiors too. And I sympathize with you having to deal with us down here. I hate dealing with other agencies, but it's part of the job. I know most of the Tacoma P.D. guys, but Seattle? Forget about it. I tell them I'm with Puyallup Tribal P.D. and I might as well be saying 'mall cop.'"

Brunelle winced at the truth of that statement. "Yeah, well, it's a small police department. I'm sure other small departments get the same reaction."

Sixrivers stared at Brunelle for several seconds. "You really think that's true?"

Brunelle sighed. "No, probably not. Hell, I didn't even know you had your own department until this case."

Sixrivers nodded again. "Yeah, that's what I figured."

Brunelle shrugged. "Sorry."

The detective waved it away. "Don't be. I like our department. We're small, but we serve an important function. We're close to the community. They trust us. Even the criminals. We might be on opposite sides with the NGBs when it comes to drive-bys or burglaries or drug trafficking, but we're on the same side if there's a party and it just kind of gets out of hand. I'm a firm believer in pointing things out to people, then letting them take care of it themselves. If they can't, well, then we can step in to help, but we're still part of the community."

Brunelle grinned. "But I'm not."

Sixrivers offered a kind of smile. "Nope. You're not."

"But I'm staying anyway."

"Well, good," Sixrivers leaned back toward his desk and slid that file back in front of him. "You seem like a good attorney. You'll make sure Quilcene is held accountable for what he did."

"I'll try," Brunelle said. Then he looked at his watch. "I better get going. Freddy will be here any minute."

"Good to know," Sixrivers said, then turned his attention back to his work. "See you around, I'm sure."

Brunelle walked through the cubicle and waited in Freddy's makeshift office. He remembered why he'd come down, and paced nervously, stewing and telling himself he must have it wrong.

"Hey, Dave!" Freddy greeted his co-counsel affably as he strolled into the room. "Good to see you. So, what's so important that I have to miss the all-you-can-eat casino buffet?"

Brunelle frowned. He'd seen Chen and the other detectives do this hundreds of times. There was an art to confronting a suspect, reading him, and drawing out the information without him being able to help himself. But Brunelle wasn't a cop. He was a prosecutor. A trial lawyer. He asked questions, people answered. The end.

"Why'd you do it, Freddy?"

Freddy cocked his head. The smile slipped a bit. "Do what?"

"Do who?" Brunelle corrected. "Quilcene's cousin. Why did you have to go and kill him?"

"What?!" Freddy threw his hands wide. "Me? Are you kidding? You have to be kidding."

Brunelle shook his head slowly. "I'm not kidding, Freddy. I wish I were."

"I didn't kill Quilcene's cousin, Dave." Freddy's voice raised in both pitch and volume. "How could you even think that? *Why* would you think that?"

"It all adds up, Freddy." He met his partner's wide-eyed

gaze. "You talk too much,.."

"Talk too much?" Freddy repeated. "What are you talking about?"

Brunelle noticed Freddy's face was flushing and his breaths were coming quicker. The smile was completely gone.

"In the casino," Brunelle started. "You told me blood feuds were a good thing. And I heard you refuse to give a statement to the cops. In your car talking to a friend, my ass. Then, in court—that argument of yours—about exactly how to carry out a blood feud in this case."

"I was exaggerating," Freddy argued, "to prove a point."

Brunelle shook his head. "Maybe the others thought that. LeClair, Talon, the gallery. But you got too close to the truth. You told me someone else from the tribe could take up the feud for Traver. Well, you're in the tribe, Freddy. Then you stood up in front of God and everybody and said someone in Quilcene's family should be killed. Killed with the same knife."

Freddy raised an enigmatic eyebrow. "Did I?"

"Yes," Brunelle growled. "And Bobby Quilcene was murdered. With the same knife"

Freddy raised an eyebrow. "Well, wasn't he dead already when I said that?"

"Yes, he was," Brunelle confirmed. "And you stole the knife out of property the day before he was killed."

"I didn't steal the knife!" Freddy insisted. "I just looked at it. Trial prep. I guess I forgot to tell you."

"It's trial prep if you look at it," Brunelle countered. "Not if you check it out and don't return it."

Freddy frowned but didn't say anything.

"It was the same knife," Brunelle repeated. "The same knife killed Traver and Bobby Quilcene."

Freddy crossed his arms. "Says who?"

"Says our M.E.," Brunelle stretched the truth a bit. "Kat Anderson."

"Kat Anderson?" Freddy's frown bounced back to his usual grin. "Oh, wow. We used to date. Say, 'Hi' for me."

"Damn it, Freddy!" Brunelle slammed the table. "You checked the knife out of property, you fucking idiot. The day before the murder. You fucking signed for it. We know you did it."

Freddy looked down and shook his head, the frown returning. "No, no, no. I didn't— Wait. Who's 'we'?"

"The case detective and I," Brunelle answered. "We went to look at the knife today and the evidence guy showed us the check out sheet with your signature on it."

Freddy shook his head again. "No, that's not right. I looked at it, but it was just a viewing. I just had the officer show it to me. She never even let go of the box it was strapped into. She just held up the box for me to see."

Brunelle stared at him, unbelieving.

"It's a really nice knife," Freddy went on. "The handle is ivory, I think. All carved and stuff."

"Freddy," Brunelle tried to keep his voice level. "You need to turn yourself in. I know you're under a lot of stress. Talon told me how you don't have a regular law job and—"

"What?!" Freddy shrieked. "You've talked to Talon about me? That bitch? Well, fuck her and her snooty law firm. I don't need them. And I don't need you or this case either. I thought it'd be great to work with you, Dave. Learn a few things. But you're just as big of an asshole as Talon, did you know that? So fuck you both. I quit."

He turned and stormed out. Between the references to Kat and Talon, Brunelle almost forgot what they we're really talking about. "Freddy! Wait. It'll go easier for you if you turn yourself in."

But Freddy didn't reply. Brunelle hurried through the cubicles, looking for an officer, any officer. He spied Sixrivers still sitting at his desk.

"Detective!" Brunelle ran to his doorframe. "You're not going to believe this, but—"

The sound of gunfire echoed through the precinct. Then squealing tires. Then nothing.

The parking lot.

Sixrivers jumped up from his desk and he and Brunelle ran out the front door, along with a half dozen other officers. The suspect vehicle was peeling out of the far end of the parking lot, way too far to get a license plate.

Turning back, Brunelle saw the result of the gunfire. On the asphalt, atop a quickly growing slick of arterial blood, was Freddy. His eyes gazed up at the darkening clouds with that lifeless stare Brunelle knew only too well.

Sixrivers knelt down to confirm what they both already knew.

"He's dead."

CHAPTER 18

Brunelle sat in Sixrivers' cramped office in the corner of the precinct. He knew he wasn't under arrest, but he also knew he wasn't free to go. Sixrivers was overseeing the collection of the body, then he needed to speak with the last person to see Freddy alive: Brunelle.

He knew he was a witness.

He knew he might be a suspect.

He knew he should lawyer up.

It was the smart thing to do. But it wasn't the right thing to do. He hadn't known Freddy long, but he considered him a friend. And his friend had just been murdered.

"Mr. Brunelle," Sixrivers finally stepped into his office. "Thank you for waiting so patiently."

The detective sat down heavily in his desk chair. It had been almost three hours since the shots rang out. Probably about that long since Sixrivers was about to clock out for the day. He looked tired. It reminded Brunelle that he felt exhausted too. It had been a long, terrible, horrible day. The ass-kicking by Talon seemed like eons ago.

Sixrivers opened his desk drawer and pulled out two things: a digital recorder and a *Miranda* advisement form. "Just a formality," he assured.

"Sure." Brunelle forced a half-smile.

Sixrivers filled out the top half of the form with the case information, Brunelle's name, date and time, etc. When he finished, he looked up like he'd just realized something.

"Are you even going to talk?" he asked.

Brunelle sighed deeply. "Yeah, I'm going to talk."

Sixrivers paused for a moment, thoughts hidden behind his dark eyes, then he reached out and turned on the recorder. "Good."

He pushed it between them. "This is Detective Thomas Sixrivers of the Puyallup Tribal Police Department. The time is now nineteen-fifty-two hours. This is the statement of David Brunelle. Mr. Brunelle, you have the right to remain silent..."

Sixrivers read each of the rights on the form into the recorder, even though they both knew them by heart. When he'd finished, Brunelle signed the form and the interrogation could begin.

Brunelle wondered whether Sixrivers might employ some of the same psychological techniques he'd seen Chen and other detectives use on suspects. Apparently not.

"Okay, Mr. Brunelle. Why don't you just tell me everything you know?"

So Brunelle explained it all. The initial murder of George Traver. The reasons Quilcene did it. The defense Talon put forward. Freddy checking the knife out of property. The murder of Quilcene's cousin. Freddy's argument in court. His comments at the casino. Brunelle confronting him. And ending with the gunfire that took Freddy's life. When he finished, Sixrivers just stared at him, chiseled chin on thick fist.

"Are you fucking kidding me?" he finally asked.

Brunelle was taken aback. He could feel his face flushing.

"No, I'm dead serious. That's exactly what happened."

Sixrivers pursed his lips into a disapproving frown. "The witnesses in the parking lot make it sound like a drive-by of the police station by the NGBs. They observed multiple males in the car, flashing gang signs as they drove away. McCloud just stepped outside at the exact wrong time."

Brunelle shook his head. "No, I'm telling you. Traver molested Quilcene's niece. Quilcene killed Traver. Freddy killed Quilcene's cousin. Now Quilcene's gang has murdered Freddy. Hell, Quilcene's out on home detention. He probably was the shooter."

Sixrivers leaned back in his chair and crossed his arms.

"I know it sounds crazy," Brunelle admitted, "but Freddy practically confessed to it in open court this morning. And if I could figure it out, Quilcene sure as hell could have."

Sixrivers tapped his chin for several seconds. Then he leaned forward and turned off the recorder.

"I think we're done," he announced.

Brunelle looked Sixrivers in the eye. "You're not going to follow up on this, are you?"

The detective met his gaze, then stood up. "I said we're done. You can go now, Mr. Brunelle."

Brunelle stood up too. "I'm telling you—"

"Goodbye, Mr. Brunelle," Sixrivers interrupted. "You really don't belong here. Maybe you should go back up to Seattle and let someone else worry about Quilcene."

Brunelle was about to argue, then he remembered that's all he'd wanted since Duncan had first explained the arrangement to him. Maybe he could finally get his wish.

CHAPTER 19

"No."

Duncan was firm. The morning sun shone across his desk, giving him an aura of divine righteousness as he denied Brunelle's plea to get off the case.

"I'm sorry, Dave, but no way. This is your case. You know how big a deal this is. Everybody will be watching this trial. I can't give it to just anyone, especially not at this late juncture. I'm counting on you."

Brunelle threw his hands up at the 'I'm counting on you' card. "Come on, Matt. This thing has spun totally out of control. I'm a witness to two murders, for Christ's sake."

"Eh, not really," Duncan replied. "You didn't actually see the murders. You just came up afterward."

"Immediately afterward," Brunelle argued.

"Just a difference in timing," Duncan countered. "You came up on the first murder too, just a lot later."

"I came up on Traver's murder because Chen called me at one in the fucking morning. These two happened while I was right there. I heard the gunshots."

Duncan paused. "I thought Quilcene's cousin was stabbed."

Brunelle pinched the bridge of his nose. "That's not really the point. I heard Quilcene's cousin scream. I watched Freddy's killer speed away."

"Good," Duncan assured evenly. "I'm sure you'll be a great witness for the Pierce County Prosecutor's Office, if they ever catch who did it. But right now, I need you to be a great prosecutor for the King County Prosecutor's Office."

Brunelle looked down and ran his hands through his hair, but wasn't sure what to say.

"Just stay focused," Duncan advised. "Those other murders are just like the other cases in your file cabinet. Unrelated homicides. Focus on what's in front of you."

Brunelle looked up. "But what if they're not unrelated?"

Duncan's face screwed up into a frown. "What do you mean? A gang member with a hundred enemies, and a lawyer in the wrong place at the wrong time. Of course they're unrelated."

Brunelle frowned. "I don't know, Matt. Traver had no family. Freddy said the blood feud could continue if someone else took up the cause. What if Freddy really did take it up? What if he really did stab Quilcene's cousin? That would explain why he was killed."

Duncan returned Brunelle's frown. "I don't buy it, Dave. But so what? By the time the cops unravel it, you'll be done with the Quilcene trial."

"So what?" Brunelle complained. "So I'm the other prosecutor. If Freddy took up the feud for our victim, then I'm pretty sure I'm on Team George too."

Duncan stared at Brunelle for several seconds. "That's crazy, Dave."

"I know, I know. But this whole damn thing is crazy."

Duncan nodded. "Okay, fine. You're Team George. So what?"

"So I'm in the goddamn blood feud now, that's what."

"Good," Duncan grinned.

"Good?" Brunelle shook his head at Duncan. "What's good about that?"

"Well, they made the last move," Duncan explained. "As long as you don't kill anyone on their team, you should be fine."

Brunelle thought about it for a moment, then started nodding. "Okay, yeah. That makes sense."

"Unless another one of Quilcene's family happens to get offed in random gang violence and they think you did it."

Brunelle's shoulders dropped. "Oh, great. What do I do if that happens.?"

Duncan smiled darkly. "Get co-counsel."

Brunelle shook his head. "Great. Thanks, Matt. Very helpful."

He stood up and headed for the door.

"Hey, Dave?" Duncan called out after him.

Brunelle turned around. "Yeah?"

"Maybe the best cure for Team George is a Team Dave."

Brunelle narrowed his eyes, not understanding.

"It's okay to have people on your team, Dave," Duncan explained. "You've got lots of friends. Lean on them if you have to."

Brunelle considered for a moment. "Okay, Matt. Thanks." Then he turned and walked out, giving the doorframe a light punch as he passed.

CHAPTER 20

Kat's office was the last one on the left. Just off the examining room. Brunelle could never understand how she could sit at a desk so close to the stench of death. He supposed she must not even notice it any more.

"Knock, knock," he said as he tapped on her doorframe. "Surprise."

She looked up from her computer and took in the sight of him. Her expression was difficult to decipher. Either she was happy to see him then tried to hide it, or she was happy to see him then changed her mind.

"Oh. It's you." She turned back to her screen. "Who let you in?"

"Jody," Brunelle replied. "Homicide prosecutors get waved right in."

"Pity," Kat said without looking at him. "They should be more careful."

Brunelle shifted his weight. "Look." He rubbed the back of his neck. "I just wanted to say I'm sorry. This case has gotten under my skin and, um, well: sorry."

Kat finally looked away from her monitor. She spun in her seat to fully face him. "Sorry, huh? Sorry for what?"

There was an unmistakable edge to her voice.

"Um," Brunelle started. "Sorry it seemed like I was using you to review autopsy reports for me the other night."

Kat nodded. "Uh huh." She pursed her lips. "Seemed like?"

Brunelle frowned. "Right." He cast his eyes downward. "I'm sorry I *did* use you to review autopsy reports for me the other night."

Kat offered another small nod. Then she just sat there. After a few moments, she spread her hands. "Anything else?"

"Uh, well," Brunelle stammered, "like I said, this case has really gotten to me and—"

"No, dumbass," Kat interrupted. "Anything else you're sorry for?"

"Uh...." Brunelle felt a dump of adrenaline. This was going deeper than he'd planned. "I'm sorry I did it over dinner?" he tried. "When we were supposed to be having a date."

Kat's eyes narrowed. "No, not that. Jesus, David..." She crossed her arms and shook her head. "How about you're sorry you haven't called me for four months? How about you're sorry you made me think we had something special when I guess we really didn't? Or, if we did, then how about you're sorry you didn't follow up on it? How about you're sorry you made me think I was just another woman you charmed to get whatever it was you wanted? How about you're sorry for not returning my calls, or replying to my emails, or acknowledging me at all? Not even a curt, rude, 'Busy. Will call soon.' How about you're sorry for leaving it to me to explain to my daughter why this really great guy suddenly disappeared? How about you're sorry for being a complete asshole and treating me like garbage? How about that?"

Brunelle was dumbstruck. The adrenaline dump proceeded in earnest and his mind raced to catch up with his feelings. He just stood there.

"Um," he said finally. "Yeah, that. Sorry about all that too."

Kat sneered and shook her head again. "Wow. Really? That's the best you can do? 'Sorry for all that too'? Damn it, David, I thought you were better than that. I guess not."

She turned back to her work.

Brunelle ran a hand over his head. "Uh, look. I— Um…" He caught himself and took a deep breath. "I was scared."

Kat scoffed. "Scared?" she repeated derisively without looking back at him. "Well, I'm sorry that needy Miss Kat scared little David."

"No, no. Not scared by you. For you." When Kat still didn't look at him, he added, "And Lizzy."

That had the desired effect. Kat turned to glare at him. "Lizzy?"

Brunelle finally stepped all the way into the office and sat in the one plastic guest chair Kat had managed to jam into the closet-like space. "Look," he said, gazing down. "You're an M.E. You chop up bodies that are already dead and testify about what killed them. If it weren't for evidence rules, I wouldn't even need you to testify about that. Any moron knows that when you get shot in the head three times, you die. But I can't argue that in closing unless a witness actually says it out loud. And only an expert can give an opinion as to cause of death. So fine, I call you, you get out of this cheery office for an afternoon, and that's the end of it for you."

He paused and looked at her.

"At least, that's supposed to be the end of it. But I don't deal with dead bodies. I deal with live bodies. Defendants. Murder defendants, who have no qualms about making more dead bodies.

"After out last case together, I realized I didn't understand that well enough. I don't have kids. You do. Believe me, there are plenty of times I picked up the phone to call you. Not a night went by that I didn't want to drive over to your place. But I thought of Lizzy and I just couldn't do it."

Kat listened expressionless. She stared at him for a few more seconds, her expression still inscrutable. "You expect me to believe that?"

Brunelle shrugged. "I don't know. Believe it or don't. It's the truth."

Another few seconds of Kat staring at him. Finally, she said, "Really?"

Brunelle ventured a tentative smile. "Really. I'm sorry, Kat. I'm sorry I made you feel like I wasn't interested, or that you weren't worth it. I just—"

"You should have told me, David," Kat said softly. "You can talk to me, you know. I have ears."

Brunelle smiled more fully. "And what lovely ears they are."

Kat crossed her arms. "Is this the part where you try to charm me?"

Brunelle allowed himself a small laugh. "No, this is the part were I use flattery to deflect the conversation from deep emotional topics I'm not comfortable discussing."

Kat surrendered her own laugh. "Bravo, sir."

Brunelle affected a bow. "Thank you, milady."

Kat's mouth twisted into a reluctant frown, but her eyes softened. "So we're okay?"

Brunelle nodded. "Yeah, we're okay. But I'm going to worry. That's just going to have to be a part of it."

"Good." Kat smiled.

"Good?" Brunelle cocked his head.

"Yes, good." Her smile broadened. "Worrying means you care."

"I worry, therefore I care," Brunelle said. "Very Cartesian."

Kat laughed. "'Cartesian'? Wow. Huge word."

Brunelle flashed a grin. "This is the part where I try to impress you with my intellect in order to avoid deep emotional topics I'm not comfortable discussing."

Kat shook her head. "Okay, okay, Mr. Sensitive. I won't get greedy. That was more of a heartfelt apology than I even thought you were capable of."

Brunelle lowered his eyebrows. "Thanks. I think."

"So, shall we try for dinner again?" Kat asked. "Just you and me and no autopsy reports on smartphones?"

"Sounds good," Brunelle was quick to answer. "This Saturday?"

"Make it Friday," Kat replied.

"Why?"

"Because I said so," Kat purred. "You're not in charge, David. Get used to it."

Brunelle rubbed his chin. "Okay. Whatever you say, boss. Dinner. Friday. I'll pick you up at six."

"Five-thirty."

Brunelle grimaced, but it slipped quickly into a true smile as he met her eyes. "Sure, boss. Five-thirty. See you then."

"See you then," Kat confirmed.

Brunelle started to walk out when Kat added, "David?"

He turned back. "Yeah?"

She shrugged and smiled. She had the best smile. "Thanks for stopping by."

Brunelle smiled back. "No problem. Glad I did. See you Friday."

And as he walked down the hallway, he patted himself on the back for not asking Kat to pull strings to get Freddy's autopsy report. That would have ruined it.

He just had to figure out how to ask it on Friday.

CHAPTER 21

Part II of Team David had to wait for the next day when Brunelle clacked down the same basement hallway beneath the Seattle P.D. headquarters. Chen pushed himself up from his spot leaning on the evidence room's front counter.

"We have to stop meeting like this," he quipped.

"Beats standing over a dead body in the rain," Brunelle replied as he reached the counter.

Chen shrugged. "Depends on what you're into."

"I'm into dry," Brunelle said. "Thanks for making time to go through the evidence with me. It shouldn't take more than an hour or so, but it's gotta get done. The omnibus hearing is in two weeks."

"Can't you lawyers speak English?" Chen teased. "Why do they call it an 'omnibus' hearing?"

Brunelle rolled his eyes. "I don't know. I think 'omni' is Latin for everything. When I first started, an old lawyer told me it was the hearing where the judge made sure everything was on the bus and the bus is ready to leave the station. All pretrial motions are done, witness lists exchanged, witness interviews completed. Everything. So trial can start as scheduled, with no lawyers asking for a continuance because the dog ate their homework."

Chen raised an eyebrow. "And how much of all that have you done yet?"

"None of it," Brunelle groaned. "Except maybe an awkward half-assed interview of the defense's star 'the-bastard-deserved-it' witness."

"The bastard did deserve it," Chen said.

"And you can shut up now," Brunelle shot back amicably. "Let's focus on what we're here to do, not on why we shouldn't bother. Evidence viewing. It's the first thing I do. You never know what you might find, and you want to lay eyes on all the shit people are going to talk about in their interviews."

"Makes sense," Chen replied. He tapped on the plexiglass. "Detective Chen and Prosecutor Brunelle here for our scheduled evidence viewing."

An evidence technician scurried to the window. This time it was a woman. Youngish, straight brown hair. "You got it, Detective. I've already put some of the items in the viewing room. You can go on in there. I'll bring in the rest in just a minute."

Chen thanked the officer and he and Brunelle walked the few feet to the evidence viewing room. They each pulled on a pair of latex gloves and Chen started thumbing through the numerous paper bags and boxes marked with only a case number and item number.

"What do you want to look at first?" he asked Brunelle.

"Let's start with the clothing," Brunelle answered. "The M.E. should have brought those over after the autopsy. I want to inspect the knife cuts. And check the pockets."

Chen referred to the property sheets then found the bags 'Items 42-44.' "Here you go. 'Clothes from autopsy.'"

"Great." Brunelle took them to the examining table, trying to decide whether to start with the cuts to the shirts or the contents of the pants pockets.

"Oh." Chen held up a lunch sack sized bag. "And here's his wallet."

Decision made. "Let's start there," Brunelle said. "Open the bag and let's see what Georgie Boy found important enough to keep in his wallet."

Chen extricated the wallet and handed it to Brunelle, who unfolded it and began extracting cards and bits of paper.

"Debit card," he called out the items as he removed them. "Grocery store receipt. Liquor store receipt. Expired glasses prescription. Bus transfer. Card from the mission."

He paused at the next one.

"What is it?" Chen asked.

Brunelle handed it to him. "It's a business card from a Seattle P.D. detective. 'James Henderson.' Why would he have that? Is that who he was supposed to register with?"

Chen frowned at the card, turning it over in his hand. "No, Henderson is one of our gang detectives. Young guy. They make the old farts pull registration duty."

"Gang detective?" Brunelle questioned. "Why would Traver have a gang detective's card?"

Chen held it up. "It's in good shape too. Not as beat up as the other crap in that wallet. He hadn't had it for long."

Just then, the evidence officer walked in with an armful of evidence bags and boxes. "Here's the rest of the stuff."

"Let me help you." Brunelle jumped in to take the less stable items off the top of the teetering pile.

"Thanks," the officer exhaled. She set her remaining load on the examining table. Brunelle went to follow suit, then noticed he was holding an oblong box labeled, "Item 1 - Knife - Biohazard."

It was too heavy to be empty.

His eyes widened. "What the hell is this?"

The officer squinted at the writing on the box. "That's the knife."

"The knife?" Chen looked up from his examination of Det. Henderson's card.

"Sure," the evidence officer replied. "Says so right there. Besides, I recognize the box."

Brunelle looked at Chen, then back at the young officer. "You recognize the box?"

"Yeah," she explained. "Another prosecutor came to look at it a while back. He didn't bring a detective like you, so I just went ahead and did the viewing with him. He just wanted to see the one thing, so I figured it would be okay."

She pointed to some red evidence tape on the box. "See, those are my initials from when I resealed it after the viewing."

Brunelle closed his eyes and pinched the bridge of his nose. "We were here a few days ago and the evidence officer then told us that the knife had been checked out and never returned."

The officer frowned. "No, it never left. Although I had a heck of a time finding it just now. Somebody misplaced it with an entirely different case. An arson investigation from six months ago—still unsolved."

"Why would he say it was checked out and not returned?" Chen pressed.

The officer picked up the original property sheets from the table and examined them. "He probably just misread my stamp. If it's just a quick viewing and the item never leaves the front area, I only have them sign once. Just to show that it was looked at. There's no chain of custody issue because it never left my hands. So, really, why have them sign twice?"

"Why have them sign twice?" Brunelle almost shouted. "I'll tell you wh—"

"Understood, officer," Chen stepped in. "Thanks for explaining that. Do you remember anything else about the viewing? Did the other prosecutor say anything?"

The young woman took a moment to pull suspicious eyes from the still-glaring Brunelle. "Not really," she answered. "He didn't even touch it. He just had me hold it up to him so he could see the handle. It was a really nice handle, all intricate and carved and stuff." She paused and looked back to Brunelle. "You should look at it."

Brunelle closed his eyes again and nodded. "Yes. Yes, we should. Thanks."

Chen thanked the evidence officer too and she hurried back to her post, leaving the knife on the table.

Brunelle opened his eyes and laid a finger lightly on the box. "Damn it," he whispered.

Chen put a hand on his shoulder. "Agreed."

CHAPTER 22

Sure enough, the knife was in the box, still strapped in with the original zip-ties. The handle was impressive indeed. Ivory and covered in Native American carvings and inscriptions, the significance of which Brunelle and Chen could only guess.

Brunelle added 'Native American murder weapon carved handle expert' to his mental witness list. Then they plodded through the rest of the evidence viewing. Brunelle tried to focus on the task at hand, but couldn't help but recall how fervently Freddy had denied taking the knife. And how fervently Brunelle had insisted he had.

But after the initial excitement of the gang detective's business card, and the horror of the not-missing knife, the evidence viewing revealed little of interest. They pulled off their gloves and called for the evidence officer to repackage the items.

Then they went upstairs to meet Detective James Henderson.

"Jimmy Henderson," the detective introduced himself as he shook Brunelle's hand. "Nice to meet you. Larry says you do homicides, so I guess it was just a matter of time 'til we met."

He wasn't all that young, but definitely a few years junior to Brunelle and Chen. Brunelle guessed thirty-five or so. He sported a shaved head, a neat goatee, and muscles that practically ripped the seams of his shirt. His office was decorated in a mix of pirated gang-thug photos and mixed martial arts trophies.

"What can I do for you gentleman?" Henderson asked as they all sat down in the small office.

Brunelle got right to it. "George Traver. Old, homeless, Native American guy."

Henderson tapped his lips. "Yeah, I know him. Long hair? Heavy-set dude?"

"Dead dude," Brunelle answered. "I didn't really notice his hair when I was standing over him with a knife sticking out of his chest."

Henderson frowned and slapped the arm of his chair. "Really? Damn. I kinda liked him. I wondered why I hadn't heard from him in a bit."

"You kinda liked him?" Chen screwed up his face. "He was a child molester. And a registered sex offender who hadn't registered in over six months."

Henderson nodded. "Yeah, I sort of had to overlook that."

Brunelle raised a hand. "Wait, wait. You had to overlook it? You hadn't heard from him in a while? What's going on? Why did this guy have your card in his wallet?"

Henderson slapped his forehead. "He had my card in his wallet? God, no wonder he got offed."

Brunelle grabbed his own temples. "Okay, hold on." He lowered his hand again. "I'm having a really bad day. I discovered a friend of mine didn't do what I thought he did and I'm still grappling with the fact that he's dead now because of the manner, place, and time I chose to confront him about it. So, if you could just do me a favor and explain, slowly and clearly, why George Traver had your card in his wallet."

Henderson looked to Chen, with an obvious 'Is this guy nuts?' look. Chen returned a 'He's okay; just answer his question' nod and Henderson shrugged.

"George was just another homeless guy in Pioneer Square," Henderson said. "I found him drunk and disorderly one night and ran him for warrants. The failing to register thing showed up. I was going to arrest him when he told me he knew about me, about how all the gangbangers talk about 'Henderson' and are scared of me, and he could help me get some of them."

Henderson paused. Brunelle supposed he wanted some acknowledgement of being feared throughout the Seattle gang community. When he didn't get it, he went on.

"At first, I didn't buy it," he said. "But then he told me he was Native and he'd heard the NGBs—" He stopped and looked to Brunelle. "You know the Native Gangster Bloods?"

"I'm familiar with them," Brunelle replied dryly. "Keep going."

"Right. The NGBs were looking to expand from Tacoma up to Seattle. He said he knew all the NGBs and could keep tabs on them for me if I just didn't arrest him."

"So you didn't arrest him," Chen confirmed. "Instead, you made him a snitch."

Henderson nodded, a satisfied smile in the corner of his mouth.

"And now he's dead," Brunelle observed. "So that didn't work out so well for him."

"It clears the warrant," Henderson joked.

Brunelle offered a pained smile. Then a light bulb went off.. His smile grew wider and he stood up. "Thank you, Detective

Henderson. You've made me a very happy man."

"Oh," he replied, standing up as well. "Why is that?"

"Because now I have an excuse to drop in on a very mean, but very attractive defense attorney and tell her I'm going to kick her ass."

CHAPTER 23

"Ms. Winter will see you now," the young male receptionist announced, standing to guide Brunelle back into the opulent bowels of Gordon, High and Steinmetz.

Finally, Brunelle thought. He'd scheduled the appointment for 3:30. He looked at his watch as he stood up. 4:28. He figured for the first fifteen minutes she might actually have been busy, but the rest was just to make him wait. To show him who was in charge.

But he needed to get this information to her ASAP. And he wanted to be there to see her face when she got it. When he'd called, the secretary had insisted that Talon was booked with court appearances and client appointments until late Friday.

"Fine," he'd said. "Late Friday. What time?"

3:30, she'd said. Or, as it turned out, 4:30.

He followed the receptionist down the cherry furniture lined hallways. Although it was approaching 5:00, not one of the desk-ridden attorneys looked like they'd be going home anytime soon.

Talon was no exception. She sat at her desk typing maniacally, her long black hair sliding down the back of her golden silk blouse.

"Dave," she greeted him without pulling her eyes from her screen. "Hold on. Just let me finish this paragraph."

Her familiarity—friendliness even—surprised him. He liked it. "Uh, sure," he replied and sat in one of her luxurious office chairs. Her firm had the top floor of one of Tacoma's few office towers. Her particular office had a panoramic view of Commencement Bay to the left and Mount Rainier to the right. Brunelle busied himself appraising the prints and diplomas and certificates decorating her office walls as Talon's fingers pounded out the last few words of whatever she was working on.

"There!" She threw her hands up from the keyboard. "Done."

"Is that a love note for me?" Brunelle joked, meaning a motion or a brief on their case. He instantly regretted it.

"You wish." Talon smirked at him. "I've got more than our little case. We're suing the biggest corporation in Washington and this brief is going to give their lawyers a fucking heart attack."

Her smirk blossomed into a full-blown smile, showing off those perfect teeth of hers. "Yours isn't the only ass I'm going to kick."

Brunelle nodded politely, but growing tired of the refrain. "Yeah, about that. I'm afraid I have some new information on the case."

He reached into the file he'd brought with him and dropped Henderson's hastily drafted report on her desk. "Hot off the press. Read all about it."

Talon glanced at it just long enough to recognize it as a police report. She folded her hands on top of it and looked at Brunelle. "All about what?"

"All about your client's real motive," Brunelle replied with his own smarmy smile. "The one that's going to blow your bullshit blood revenge claim right out of the water."

Talon smiled, like a mongoose meeting a cobra. "You think so, huh? Well, then. Let's see what you've got here, Dave."

He tried to ignore that hearing her say his name—rather than 'jackass'—was a very pleasant sensation indeed. He looked down at his hands while she began reading the police report.

Those damn age spots were still there.

He raised his eyes and appraised her office. It was clean and orderly, with just enough clutter to show she was working on a hell of a lot—all at once.

Talon finally looked up from the report. "I thought you said you had bad news for me?"

Brunelle huffed at her bravado. "Damn right I do. My victim was a snitch. Snitching out your guy's gang."

Talon nodded. "Yeah, I kind of already knew that."

"You did?" Brunelle was stunned. "How the hell did you know that? I just found out."

"That's because you're on the outside looking in," Talon explained. "But I'm already inside. Tell me, how did you figure it out?"

Brunelle leaned back into the soft chair. "Well, I was looking through the evidence with Detective Chen. We went through Traver's wallet and found the business card for a Seattle gang detective, James Henderson. When we met with Henderson he explained he'd recruited Traver as a snitch."

Talon grinned. "Wow, that was a lot of work. Wanna know how I found out?"

Brunelle crossed his arms. "How?"

"Traver," she leaned back too, but it was so she could show off her smugness, "was a drunk and a loser. And a really lousy snitch. He told anyone who would listen that he was working with the cops. My client and a half dozen other family members told me about Traver being a snitch the first time I met with them."

Brunelle dropped his arms to his side. "And you didn't think that was worth mentioning to me?"

Talon actually laughed. "Of course not, Dave. Come on. You know how discovery works in a criminal case. You have to tell me everything, and I don't have to tell you shit. Pardon my French."

Somehow, hearing her swear made Brunelle's heart race almost as much as the constant use of his first name.

"Okay, fine." Brunelle regained himself. "You knew and I didn't. But now I do and so will the jury."

"Good," Talon smiled.

Brunelle cocked his head. "Good? I give the jury the alternative motive for your client killing Traver and you say 'good'?"

Talon nodded. "Yep. Good." Her eyes flashed. "Why don't you tell me exactly what you'll say to the jury in closing argument?"

Brunelle thought for a moment, then sat up straight and took on the affect of a prosecutor delivering his summation. "Ladies and gentlemen, Johnny Quilcene didn't murder George Traver to avenge the molestation of his niece. He did it to silence a confidential informant. Someone who was reporting to the police about the illegal activities of the Native Gangster Bloods, the very street gang Johnny Quilcene belonged to. Quilcene murdered George Traver not because of what he had done, but rather because of what he threatened to do in the future: bring down the NGBs. There's a saying in the criminal community: 'snitches are bitches who end up in ditches.' And Johnny Quilcene put George Traver in a ditch."

Talon gave a polite golf-clap. "Excellent. Really. Especially the 'snitches in ditches' part. Bravo."

Brunelle smiled despite her obvious sarcasm. "Thank you. I'd hoped you would approve."

Talon's smile remained as her eyes narrowed. "Wanna hear mine?"

Brunelle crossed his arms again and leaned back. "By all means."

Talon took a deep breath. Brunelle couldn't help but look at her rising chest for a moment before managing to pull his eyes up.

"Ladies and gentlemen," she started, her voice a notch lower—and sexier—than usual, "you just heard the prosecutor refer to the tragic loss of human life as 'snitches are bitches who end up in ditches.'"

Brunelle bristled, but didn't interrupt. He knew there was no way he was going to use that phrase now in his actual closing argument.

"It's catchy," she went on, speaking past him to an imaginary box full of jurors, "kind of funny, and it rhymes. What more could anyone want for an explanation of why one human being would kill another? Well, how about reality? How about complicated, messy, terrible reality? Let's talk reality. George Traver really molested three-year-old Caitlyn Quilcene. With his own filthy, disgusting, real hands. And she really will never forget those terrible things that really happened to her. And George Traver really was a registered sex offender. He really was supposed to check in with the police every week so they—and we—could monitor his activity. And he really stopped registering. And that's really a crime. It's called Failing to Register as a Sex Offender. He really committed it and there was a real warrant out for his arrest. A real piece of paper signed by a real judge who really said go arrest that vile piece of garbage before he hurts someone again.

"And then you know what happened? What really, actually, unbelievably happened? A real cop—a real detective—really found George Traver. He really knew what Traver had done and what he was capable of doing again. And he really knew about the real warrant that the real judge had issued because everyone knew that George Traver was really going to hurt a real person if he wasn't stopped. And you know what the real cop really did? He really let George Traver go.

"He didn't arrest him. He didn't even make him start registering again. He didn't say, 'Hey, George, go turn yourself in and clear out these warrants and start registering again and then you can help me. No, he really just walked away. He gave that real child molester his business card and walked away. The police just walked away. Really.

"Ladies and gentleman, if the authorities had done their job, George Traver would never have laid a hand on Caitlyn. He would have been arrested, charged with failing to register, and sent off to prison. Really.

"Then they come back and say, 'We know we didn't do what we were supposed to do. We know we had every chance to save Caitlyn from that terrible fate. We know we didn't protect her. We know we didn't do our jobs. We know we didn't do anything. But don't you do anything either. Just take it. Really. Like Caitlyn did when George Traver laid his filthy hands on her. Just take it.'"

Brunelle's heart sank.

Talon wasn't smiling any more. She was in the zone. Not just arguing her point like any lawyer could, but truly feeling the force behind her words. Slowly, she came back to the surface and her eyes focused on Brunelle again.

"Fuck," Brunelle exhaled.

Her smile returned. "Exactly. I told you, Dave. I'm already three steps ahead of you."

"I can see that," he managed to reply.

"And I'm gonna kick your ass."

He sighed. "Yeah, I can see that too."

Talon looked at the antique-style clock on her bookshelf. It was almost 5:00. "You up for a cup of coffee?" she asked suddenly. "I'm buying. I wanna talk some more with you."

Brunelle's head was still thick from the power of Talon's mock closing. "Uh, sure." He stood up as Talon did too. "What do you want to talk about?"

Talon took her coat off the back of her office door. A bright red raincoat. Stunning. Of course.

"I'll tell you when we get there. But it'll be worth the wait." She winked. "Really."

CHAPTER 24

Talon led Brunelle the few short blocks to her favorite coffee house. She picked a window seat so they could watch the bumper-to-bumper traffic grind its way down the hill toward the freeway.

"I always grab a cup of coffee this time of day," she explained as they sat down with their drinks, her treat. "There's something about seeing all these people going home that motivates me to get back to work."

Brunelle looked at the cars then at her. "You're not kidding, are you?"

She sipped her coffee and smiled. "Nope."

Brunelle drank from his too. "Well, you've got the killer lawyer routine down pat. I'll admit I'm impressed."

Talon nodded. "Good. You should be."

Brunelle shook his head amicably. "You know, it's almost too bad we're on opposite sides. I think we might make a good team."

"Who says we aren't?" Talon replied over her coffee.

"Um." Brunelle thought a moment. "I'm pretty sure we aren't. I'm prosecuting your client. Not a whole lot of room for collaboration there."

Talon waved the idea away. "Of course there is. Let's settle this case. Right now, over coffee. The only thing keeping us from being together is this case. So let's get rid of it."

Brunelle didn't fail to notice that Talon said 'being together' rather than 'working together.' He was speechless for a moment as his heart restarted, so Talon went on.

"First degree manslaughter," she said. "I'll plead him out first thing in the morning. Then we're done."

Brunelle sipped at his coffee, knowing he was going to say 'No', but not in any hurry to end their conversation.

"You know it's a fair resolution," Talon pressed. "It's like those old fashioned 'hot blood' cases where the guy comes home to find his wife in bed with another man. Even though he kills her intentionally, we say it's manslaughter, not murder. That's because we understand, sometimes people just lose it. And justifiably so.

"My guy lost it too. And justifiably so. So give him a manslaughter, and that lets you and me both be done with the one thing we can't work together on."

Brunelle tapped his finger against his lips. "Well..." he said slowly. "The standard range is seven to nine years on a manslaughter one. If we agreed to high end..."

"Oh no," Talon interjected. "No agreement on the sentence. I'm going to argue for no jail."

"Are you kidding?" Brunelle dropped his hand from his face. "Low end is seven years. How are you—?"

"Low end under Washington law," Talon grinned. "But I'll be arguing for a sentence under tribal law. It is the tribal court after all."

"He's charged under Washington law," Brunelle pointed out.

Talon's smile grew. "And that will be my first issue on appeal. What gives you the authority to charge under *your* statute in *my* court?"

Brunelle just stared at her.

"Wanna hear my other appeal issues?" she teased. "I'm actually about nine steps ahead of you."

Brunelle wasn't sure what to say, but before he could think of anything, his phone rang. Glad for the interruption, he pulled it out and looked at the screen.

It was Kat.

"Fuck."

"Not on the first date," Talon quipped. "And not right after coffee. And certainly not when I bought."

Brunelle ran his hand through his hair and squinted his eyes shut. "No, not that kind of fuck. I forgot something. Something important."

He stared at the phone for another second then decided he better answer it. He stood up and stepped away from Talon, suddenly realizing how loud the coffee shop chatter was.

"Hello? This is Dave Brunelle." As if he didn't know who was calling.

"Hello, Dave Brunelle," came the throaty voice on the other end. "This is Kat Anderson. Where the heck are you?"

Brunelle looked at his watch. 5:41.

"Uh, Tacoma," he stammered. "I got stuck in Tacoma. Uh, working on this damn case."

There was a long pause. "You're standing me up?"

Brunelle ran that hand through his hair again. "Well, um, it's not like I wanted to, or planned on it or anything. It's just that I got stuck down here."

"Wow," Kat said. "You stood me up."

"Look, let's just reschedule. I wanted to do tomorrow night anyway. Would that work? Or maybe next weekend?"

"You didn't even call me to tell me you weren't coming. I had to call you."

"I know, I know." Brunelle looked across the shop at Talon. She was watching his every move. "Next weekend, okay?"

No response.

"Okay?" he tried again.

"Sure, David," Kat finally said, but Brunelle could hear the crack in her voice. "I have to go now," she said and hung up.

Brunelle didn't argue against the click. Instead, he stared at the phone for a few seconds then returned to his table with Talon.

"Girlfriend?" she asked.

Brunelle shook his head. "No," he decided.

"Not a wife," Talon said. "I already checked your finger."

Brunelle looked down at his naked left hand. "Did you?" Somehow that made him feel better. "No, not a wife. It's… It's complicated."

Talon laughed a little. Damn, he liked her laugh.

"Look, Dave," she said. "You know I'm not stupid, right?"

Brunelle raised his eyebrows. "Of course I know that. You're anything but stupid. In fact, you seem pretty fucking smart. Pardon my French."

Talon nodded. "Pardoned. Now…" She leaned back and gestured at her body with her hands. "Have you noticed that I'm rather physically attractive? Maybe not the most beautiful woman on the planet, but pretty enough?"

Brunelle tried to avoid blushing. "You're attractive," he conceded. "Sure. I suppose I noticed."

Talon shook her head at him. "You *suppose* you noticed. Okay. Well, look. If you noticed it, and I'm not stupid, don't you think I know it too?"

Brunelle hadn't really thought about it that way.

"Dave, you were about to give my client a manslaughter deal just because you think I'm hot and you were hoping you might get to nail me."

Brunelle sat up indignantly. "I was not!" *Not* 'just *because'* *anyway,* he thought.

Talon laughed again, but this time Brunelle didn't like the laugh at all. "You sure as hell were. If your girlfriend hadn't called, I I would've unbuttoned the top button on my blouse and had you agreeing to no jail time either."

Brunelle knew he was blushing now; he could feel his face burning. He was embarrassed and angry and he didn't even know what else. Of all the things he could have said, he chose, "She's not my girlfriend."

Talon smirked and shook her head. "Not if you keep acting like this."

CHAPTER 25

The next week dragged on as Brunelle filled his days trying to interview witnesses and otherwise prepare for the omnibus hearing, while filling his nights with picking up his phone to call Kat, only to set it down again. Both endeavors proved mostly fruitless.

It was becoming increasingly clear that his case would be one consisting almost entirely of professional witnesses: detectives, forensic officers, the medical examiner, etc. Whatever lay witnesses there had been to the actual killing were homeless, transient, and in the wind. It meant he might not get a description of the argument that led up to the stabbing but, on the bright side, all of his witnesses would honor their subpoenas, arrive on time, and probably not be drunk when they testified.

Still, he didn't like leaving that detail blank for Quilcene to fill in any way he pleased after Brunelle had rested his case, so he recruited Henderson to beat the bushes and scare up at least one witness who had given both a description of the murder and enough personal information to be tracked down. When Henderson had resisted—claiming too much of his own work to do—Brunelle gave him a taste of Talon's closing and he meekly agreed to help.

Connecting with Kat had been similarly frustrating. But it
was his own fault. He tried to call her cell on Saturday but had been
forced to leave a voicemail. When she didn't call back, he concluded
she didn't want to talk. A convenient conclusion, he knew. So on
Friday he sent an email to her work account confirming their
'meeting' the next day. They hadn't even discussed the details of
their date, a fact of which he was reminded when Kat emailed back,
almost immediately, 'Where and when is our *meeting*, Mr.
Brunelle?'

'University District,' he typed backed. 'Donatello's on the
Ave. 5:00 pm.'

A few seconds later: 'Fine. But if you stand me up again, I'll
demonstrate a reckless Y-incision on your torso.'

Brunelle was actually glad for the threat, because it was also
a joke. Which meant she wasn't angry any more. Or at least not as
angry. He was also glad she hadn't balked at the suggestion of a
restaurant in the U District. It dovetailed perfectly with his other
plans for the day.

He needed an expert on Native American culture, and
specifically blood revenge and criminal justice customs. The
University of Washington boasted an entire department on Native
American studies and he had managed to convince one of the
professors to meet with him about the case. If all went well,
Brunelle would be able to call him as a witness to debunk Talon's
justifiable homicide claim.

He could think a few steps ahead too.

It had an authoritative ring to it: William O'Brien, Ph.D.,
Professor of Native American Studies at the University of
Washington.

"Call me Bill," O'Brien said as he shook Brunelle's hand in
the café above the university's natural history museum.

"Dave," replied Brunelle and they both sat down at the small table O'Brien had staked out for them. Brunelle had arrived early and spent the last half hour touring the museum's Native American exhibit. It was interesting enough, he supposed, but it skewed toward artifacts and dioramas of everyday life. No mention of prevailing criminal justice systems. Another reason to go straight to source.

Well, *a* source anyway.

O'Brien was about Brunelle's age, with a thick mop of wavy strawberry blond hair, trendy glasses, and a white cable-knit sweater.

"How can I help you, Dave?"

So Brunelle explained the case. Simply, but adequately, focusing on what Traver did to Quilcene's niece and Talon's confidence in her blood revenge defense. O'Brien took it all in quietly, nodding and offering the occasional, "Ah" or, "mm-hmm." When Brunelle finished, O'Brien leaned back and rubbed his hands together.

"Oh, this is amazing," he said. "Fantastic, really. I'm so glad you called me."

"So you think you can help my case?" Brunelle confirmed.

O'Brien grinned. "Well, I don't know about that, counselor. I can give you information. Whether it's helpful to you or not, you'll have to decide."

"Fair enough," Brunelle replied. "My first question is about blood revenge generally. It was a part of Native American culture, right?"

"Well, to begin with," O'Brien took off his glasses and rubbed the lenses with his sweater, "there's no such thing as a monolithic Native American culture. Every nation, every tribe had its own history and customs, often greatly influenced by their geography and the available natural resources. For example, in the Plains where it takes great effort by many members of a tribe to take down just one buffalo, conflict and war was more common than, say, here in the Pacific Northwest where seafood was so plentiful that the natives had a saying: 'When the tide goes out, the table is set.' Now, if you compare that to the confederated tribes of the Northeast..."

Brunelle raised a hand to interrupt. "Right, sorry," he said. "I didn't mean to generalize."

"No worries," O'Brien replied. "Most lay people are as ignorant as you."

Brunelle raised an eyebrow at the comment.

"About the complexities of Native American culture, I mean."

Brunelle forced a smile. "Of course. So anyway... Blood revenge?"

"Ah yes." The glasses went back on and the professor leaned onto the table. "Well, you see, blood revenge was an important part of many Native American cultures. The concept was a simple one: if a member of one clan or family was killed by a member of another group, then that other group should plan for, and acquiesce to, the killing of one of their own."

"Acquiesce to?" Brunelle was intrigued by that wrinkle.

"Oh, yes," O'Brien enthused. "It was vital that the disagreement stop after just one killing. Otherwise blood revenge would become a blood feud, with devastating consequences for both sides. The entire purpose of blood revenge was to end the inequity caused by the first killing, and thereby discourage killings in the first place. In fact, in some ways, blood revenge was the foundation for all modern criminal justice systems. You should read Professor Miller's work on medieval Icelandic sagas and the law of blood feuds. It's some truly fascinating reading."

"Sure." Brunelle nodded. *Time to pursue another angle.* "Could a blood revenge killing be justified by something less than another killing?"

O'Brien frowned at him. "I don't understand. It's a retaliatory killing. It's designed to balance the unjustness of the initial killing."

"Understood." Brunelle nodded. "But what if the initial killing wasn't a killing at all? What if it was something less?"

"Something less?"

"Yes. Something terrible—horrific, even—but not a murder."

"Like a theft or something?" O'Brien ventured. "Oh, no. You couldn't kill someone just because they stole from you. Indeed, intertribal theft was actually another important cultural—"

"Sure, I get that," Brunelle interrupted, not eager for another lecture. "But what about something really serious? Like a serious assault? Or even a sexual assault?"

"Rape?" O'Brien translated. "Oh my. That's a very complicated issue. Sexual mores can be very different from culture to culture and it was no different for the various Native American nations. For example—"

"That's okay." Brunelle put up a hand. "I don't need examples. I'll make it simple. In my case, the murder victim molested the defendant's three-year old niece. He's claiming a justifiable blood revenge killing. Can he do that?"

O'Brien's shoulders dropped and he removed his glasses again. He chewed on an earpiece. "Can he do that?" he repeated. "Well, that's a difficult question..."

"Sometimes the best answer to a difficult question is the simplest one," Brunelle encouraged. "Yes or no, could you do a blood revenge killing for the molestation of a child?"

O'Brien replaced his glasses and pursed his lips. He chewed

his cheek for several moments as the gears spun behind his eyes. Finally, he said, "Maybe."

Brunelle threw his hands up. "Maybe? Jesus, I'll just put you on the stand after my lead detective and medical examiner. That should guarantee an acquittal. What the hell does 'maybe' mean?"

O'Brien sat up straight and looked down through his glasses. "It means," he crossed his arms, "that it depends."

Brunelle closed his eyes and sighed. "On what?"

"I would say," O'Brien explained, "that at the time the treaty you mentioned was adopted, it would have been very unlikely if not impossible for a blood revenge killing to have been condoned for the molestation of a child."

Brunelle raised his hands. "Okay, great. Stop there, and we're good."

O'Brien laughed and shook his head. "I can't stop there, because there's more. As I said earlier, I will tell you the truth, and you decide whether it's helpful. I would suggest you let me continue rather than hearing what I have to say for the first time on cross examination."

Brunelle had to grin at that. "Touché." He rolled his wrist at the academic. "Go on, professor."

"Yes, well, as I mentioned, sexual mores vary greatly from culture to culture. They also vary over time. I think it's safe to say that such things as child molestation are taken more seriously and punished more severely than they were, say, one hundred years ago."

Brunelle considered. "I suppose that might be true."

"And certainly," O'Brien continued, "there are sexual practices which are tolerated or even legitimized today, but which in the past were regularly met with violence, even in our lifetimes."

Brunelle frowned. "That's definitely true."

"So," O'Brien concluded, "even if blood revenge might not have been justified then for the molestation of a child, it might be justified now."

Brunelle shook his head. *Damn.* "That's what I was afraid of. I might be able to argue that if we're going to apply a one-hundred-year-old blood revenge defense, then we have to apply it as it would have been applied then." He lowered his head into his hands. "But that's going to sound pretty hollow against the backdrop of a victimized toddler."

O'Brien tapped his lips. "May I ask, what did the murderer use to kill the victim? Was it a gun?"

"No," Brunelle replied. "A knife. Why? Does that matter?"

"It might," O'Brien said. "What kind of knife?"

Brunelle winced. "Three-inch fixed blade. Ivory handle, with carvings of some sort. That probably doesn't help, huh?"

"I might need more information," O'Brien agreed. "Do you think you could let me see it?"

Brunelle grimaced as he considered the knife leaving the property room not-again. "What about a photograph?"

O'Brien nodded. "That should be adequate. I might be able to recognize the significance, if any, of the carvings."

Brunelle offered a distracted, "Sure." His mind was already processing what the professor had told him and trying to figure out how it would help, or hinder, his case.

"I think your problem," O'Brien offered, "is that yours is unquestionably a revenge killing, and while revenge killings are no longer justified, they once were."

"I just have to show," Brunelle articulated, "that this particular revenge killing wasn't justified enough."

"Quite the needle to thread," O'Brien observed. "I don't envy you."

Brunelle smiled. "Thanks. Me either."

The meeting was obviously over, but before they stood up O'Brien said, "May I ask you one last question?"

"Of course," Brunelle replied.

"You said something a moment ago that suggested your detective and medical examiner might not be helpful either. What did they say?"

Brunelle laughed a bit. "My detective said it was justified."

"Oh, dear."

"Yeah. And once my medical examiner heard what the victim had done, she changed her opinion from homicide to suicide."

"Now, that seems unlikely," O'Brien said.

"Well, she's the expert," Brunelle replied. "If anyone could hide a homicide as a suicide, it's her." He looked at his watch. "Which reminds me, I better get going. I'm having dinner with her in half an hour. If I'm late, it's my homicide she'll be passing off as a suicide."

O'Brien grinned. "Well, then, by all means, depart." He stood up. "It was nice to meet you. Thank you for discussing the case with me."

"No, thank you," Brunelle insisted as he shook the professor's hand. "You can expect a subpoena from me. I don't know if it'll help my case or not, but I think it's important the jury hears what you have to say. The truth is always a good thing."

"I'll look forward to receiving it," O'Brien replied. "Enjoy your dinner."

Brunelle considered the initial apologizing and groveling he'd need to do. "Thanks. I'll try. Goodbye, professor."

CHAPTER 26

Donatello's was packed. Upscale Italian on a Saturday night. Prime date material. Ordinarily, Brunelle might have avoided the U District on a Saturday night, but he had needed to be close to campus. Within walking distance. There was no way he was going to risk a traffic jam and stand Kat up again. He knew she wouldn't give him a third chance.

When he stepped into the restaurant and saw her, he was thankful he hadn't screwed up the second chance. She was gazing absently out the window, her shiny black hair reflecting the lights from the bar, and the glow of the table candle highlighting the angelic curves of her face. She was beautiful. And smart. And tough.

"Good evening, Dr. Anderson," Brunelle greeted her as he approached their table. "You look stunning this evening."

She looked up at him and smiled. Brunelle was glad to see the smile seemed genuinely warm. She had been genuinely angry, but she seemed willing to move on.

"Good evening, Mr. Brunelle," she replied in that cuddly voice of hers. "Glad to see you made it this time."

Brunelle sat down opposite her at the cozy table. "Yeah, sorry about that. This case is starting to get intense. Omnibus is Monday and trial starts the Monday after that."

"I know," Kat smiled. "I got my subpoena yesterday."

"Oh yeah?" Brunelle nodded. "Good to know those got out on time."

The waiter came over and took their drink orders. When he left, Kat picked up where they'd left off. "So lots to do on the big case, huh?"

Brunelle shrugged. "Yeah. I guess so. Sorry. I don't mean to bring my work home with me, so to speak."

Kat raised an eyebrow. "Slow down, lover boy. We're not married yet. Hell, we're barely able to make a dinner date work."

Brunelle smiled and nodded. "Right, right. I just don't want to bore you or complain. I was just explaining why I've been so busy lately."

Kat was quiet for a moment. "So you were in Tacoma, huh?"

Brunelle looked down quickly at the menu. "Oh. Um. Yep. 'Cause, you know, that's where the tribe is."

Another pause.

"What were you doing exactly?"

Brunelle's eyes stayed glued to the menu. "Oh, just working the case. You know, lawyer stuff."

"Lawyer stuff, huh?" Kat confirmed, with a smirk and a nod. "Were you meeting with the defense attorney?"

Brunelle finally looked up. "Hm? What's that?"

"The defense attorney," Kat repeated. "You know, the hot one? Were you meeting with her? Is that why you stood me up?"

Brunelle rubbed his chin. Several possible lies raced through his mind. 'No,' was the obvious one, followed by, 'Yes, but that was scheduled at 3:30,' thereby suggesting he was done well before she had called him. But he decided to just be honest—mostly. It was easier. Besides, he could still spin it a little.

"I guess so," he started, lowering the protective menu. Good body language, he knew. "I was supposed to meet with her at 3:30, but she made me wait an hour and I ended up being too late to make it back up to Seattle in time."

Kat nodded. "Oh, okay. I figured it was something like that." She looked down at her menu. "How was the coffee?"

"Not bad," Brunelle replied. "Just—" He stopped himself, but it was too late.

"I heard the background noise, Romeo." Kat shook her head at him. "Really, David, I don't care if you have to meet with a hot defense attorney. I don't even care if you do it over coffee. Whatever. But don't lie to me about it."

Brunelle grimaced. "Okay. Sorry. It's just… I didn't want you to think the wrong thing."

"Don't worry about what I think," Kat replied. "Just tell me the truth and let me decide what to think on my own."

Brunelle nodded. "Okay. That's fair." Then, for the umpteenth time lately, "Sorry."

Kat smiled. That wonderful, heart-dizzying smile. "You're forgiven. Besides, two can play at that game." The smile deepened. "How's my ex-boyfriend, Freddy? Does he like working with a big-time prosecutor from Seattle?"

"Oh, fuck," Brunelle gasped. "I haven't told you, have I?"

He knew his face had gone pale. He saw Kat's do the same.

"What?" she said. "What is it?"

"Freddy," Brunelle started. "He's, he's dead."

Kat blinked at him several times, her mouth contorted sickly. Then she swallowed hard. "Dead?" she repeated. "Dead how?"

"Shot," Brunelle answered numbly. "Somebody shot him."

Kat shook her head against the information. "Shot? Why would somebody shoot him? That can't be right."

"It was a drive-by," Brunelle explained. "Right outside the tribal police headquarters. He had just run outside when—"

But Brunelle stopped, remembering why Freddy had run outside.

"When what?" Kat insisted. "Why did he run outside? What happened, David? Were you there?"

"Uh, yes," Brunelle stammered. "Yes, I was there. I, um, I'd just been talking with him—about the case—when he stormed outside right when the shots were fired."

"What are you talking about?" Kat demanded. "Why would he storm out? What did you say to him? It better not have been about me."

"No, no. It wasn't about you. It was about…"

He trailed off. *How can I possibly explain?*

"It was about what, David?" Kat's voice was ice cold.

Brunelle swallowed. *Okay, you say you want the truth…*

"I thought Freddy might have been the one who murdered Quilcene's cousin."

"What?!" Kat shrieked. Patrons at nearby tables turned to look, but Kat ignored them. "Why the hell would you think that?"

"Well, the knife that killed Traver went missing from the property room," Brunelle explained. "Or rather, we thought it did. And Freddy was the one who checked it out. Or we thought he did. He went on and on in court about how a blood revenge killing was fine, but someone needed to take up the blood feud on behalf of Traver. And that 's what he and I were kind of doing by prosecuting Traver's killer. And you said the same knife killed Traver and Quilcene's cousin—"

"Whoa!" Kat flashed up a palm. "You stop right there, buster. I did *not* say it was the same knife. I said the injuries were consistent with it being the same or a similar knife. That's a big difference."

"Maybe to a pathologist," Brunelle countered, "but to this prosecutor that sounds a lot like 'the same knife.'"

"Did someone say knife?" a cheery voice came from over Brunelle's shoulder.

He turned around to see O'Brien, wearing a happy grin and holding the hand of a wife or girlfriend.

"It looks like I timed this just right," O'Brien said. He nodded to Kat. "This must be the medical examiner you said you were having dinner with. Pleasure to meet you. I'm Bill O'Brien, professor of Native American studies here at the U. Dave and I met just before your dinner date and made some plans."

Kat cast a vicious glare at Brunelle. Before he could even try to explain, O'Brien dug him in deeper.

"So anyway, the knife." He put a hand on Brunelle's shoulder. "You said it was decorative. I was thinking, there's a fine line between a justifiable blood revenge killing and a plain, old, not-justifiable murder. I would think, strangely enough, the more this was planned—the more it was premeditated, as you lawyers say— the more it was ceremonial, then the more likely it was blood revenge."

"Uh sure," Brunelle replied weekly. "That makes sense."

"Excellent," O'Brien chirped. "I'm glad you agree. Yes, if that knife was ceremonial, then that would lend credibility to the claim of blood revenge. The only thing better would be if you could show that the same weapon had been used in another such killing."

O'Brien smiled at Kat. "But I suppose that's more your area of expertise."

Kat's glare turned into an outright glower. Then she tore her dagger-casting eyes from Brunelle and looked up at O'Brien with a saccharine smile. "Why yes, it is. Mr. Brunelle and I were just discussing that. He's assembling quite a collection of expert witnesses for his case."

She lowered her eyes at him again, her own daggers glinting within. "That's why he's such a good lawyer. He knows how to get people to say whatever he wants. He's very good at using people that way."

The iciness in her voice was apparent to everyone. O'Brien's lady friend tugged his arm. "Come on, Bill. Let's get to our table. It was nice to meet you."

The academic let himself be pulled away after a last parting shot. "Nice to have met you, doctor. Impeccable timing, eh, Dave?"

Brunelle groaned affirmatively and lowered his head into his hands as they finally, mercifully departed.

"You bastard," said Kat. "This whole thing was a set up."

Brunelle's head jerked back up. "No. I swear. I did meet with him earlier today, but I did not set up him coming to our table like that."

"You obviously told him you were having dinner with the medical examiner on your case," Kat pointed out.

Brunelle nodded. "Yes, I did. But I didn't say, 'Please stop by our table and talk about the knife.'"

Kat crossed her arms. "Well, then. What did you say?"

Brunelle tried to recall the specific of his conversation with O'Brien. *Truth. She wants the truth.*

"I told him I was having dinner with the M.E. and I better not be late again because if anyone could disguise a homicide as a suicide, it would be you."

Brunelle looked for some sign that Kat thought his little joke was endearing. He got nothing.

Fuck.

After several moments, Kat began nodding. Then she stood up and dropped her napkin on the table. "Fine, Mr. Brunelle. I hope this little chance encounter helps you win your case. I hope it was worth it."

Brunelle motioned her back toward her chair. "Kat, please..."

"No," she replied. "I think we're done. Thanks for remembering to tell me that a dear friend of mine was killed because you falsely accused him of murder. I hope Professor O'Brien finds my autopsy report useful. I'll see you in court whatever fucking time my subpoena says to be there. And I'll be damned if I ever see you again after that."

Brunelle stood up. "Kat please. Don't do this."

"Don't so this?" she spat. "Me? What about you? How about you stop using people, you selfish asshole. How about you care about someone besides yourself? About more than just winning your next fucking case?"

Kat shook her head. "Damn it, David. You just messed up something that could have been really great. I'm pretty damn special. I'm smart and I'm funny and I could have really liked you. I was ready to. But you're too... too... You're too *you* to see that."

Brunelle just stood there, unsure what to say.

So Kat said it instead. "Goodbye."

And she walked away.

CHAPTER 27

The omnibus hearing was low-key. Brunelle liked to think he wasn't moody or emotional, but he could get melancholy. The blow-up with Kat had weighed on him all weekend. So when he saw Talon that morning, it added to the memory of how she'd played him the previous Friday. He just wanted to do the hearing and get out of there.

The judge went through his checklist with the attorneys.

"Has all discovery been completed?"

"Yes," and "Yes."

Are there any additional motions before trial?"

"No," and "No."

"Have all witnesses been disclosed?"

"Yes," and "Well, Your Honor…"

LeClair and Talon both looked to Brunelle.

"Actually," he continued, "the prosecution has one additional witness. Professor William O'Brien from the University of Washington. He teaches Native American studies."

Talon raised an eyebrow to the judge, who returned his own. "What will he be testifying to?" LeClair asked.

"Blood revenge," Brunelle answered. "I expect him to testify that, generally speaking, blood revenge was reserved for avenging other killings, not lesser crimes like child molestation."

Judge LeClair nodded. He raised the other eyebrow at Talon. "Any objection to the additional witness. Ms. Winter?"

Talon looked over at Brunelle. He expected her to object to adding a witness—an expert witness, no less—only one week before trial. But she just turned back to the judge. "No objection, Your Honor. We already had our own expert lined up in case Mr. Brunelle ever figured out he'd need one too."

She turned back to Brunelle and mouthed the phrase, 'Three steps ahead.'

Judge LeClair nodded. "Please exchange your experts' resumes and make them available for interviews before trial begins next Monday."

"Yes, Your Honor," and "Yes, Your Honor."

The judge looked back down at his checklist.

"Have all witnesses been subpoenaed?"

"Yes," and "Yes."

"Are there any out-of-state witnesses or special witness scheduling issues?"

"No," and "No."

The checklist wore on. Brunelle looked at his watch. He figured fifteen, maybe twenty minutes more, then the hearing would be over and he could forget about the damn case until he checked into his extended-stay motel Sunday night.

CHAPTER 28

Actually, he had plenty left to do to get ready for trial, so after the omnibus hearing, Brunelle went straight to his car. No trash talking with Talon. He ignored the mean-mugging from Quilcene. He didn't even say hi to the sort-of-receptionist on the way out. Just straight to the parking lot, right into his car, and directly to the freeway. He drove in silence all the way to Seattle, with the exception of a single phone call. An hour later he was back at the Seattle P.D. property room.

No Chen this time. The phone call had been to confirm that the evidence guys could take the photos of the knife. They could. That's all he needed.

The front window was being attended by the same woman who didn't feel the need to fill in all the blank lines on the evidence viewing stamp. She offered a "Nice to see you again," then went to fetch the knife box and a camera.

When she returned to the window, she had a strange expression on her face.

"There may be a problem," she said, sliding the box under the plexiglass to Brunelle.

Brunelle looked at the box. The evidence tape was broken and the box was sealed with plain old scotch tape. He picked it up and knew right away it was too light. He pulled it open, snapping the tape, and confirmed: this time the knife really was gone.

The evidence officer stepped away and hurried back with the master property sheets.

"No one's checked it out," she reported.

Brunelle stared at the empty box, its zip-ties cut and hanging loose. He supposed he'd be calling Chen after all.

CHAPTER 29

Sunday couldn't come soon enough. The theft of the knife was troubling—for lots of reasons—but not fatal to his case. Forensics had already photographed the hell out of it when it was first collected, so Brunelle could send those pictures to O'Brien. He could also show them to the jury, although it was going to be awkward to explain how the knife had disappeared.

Especially when he himself didn't know how. Or why. Or by whom.

But he'd leave that to Chen to find out. That's what detectives were for.

Brunelle spent the week finishing his preparations for trial. He drafted his jury instructions, composed his opening statement, and called each witness to confirm their availability. Except Kat. She wouldn't answer his calls and didn't return his voicemails. He'd been forced to have his legal assistant confirm with her by email.

As he drove down to Tacoma Sunday evening, he double checked his readiness for trial. Everything was all set. He was ready to prosecute a murder that everyone from his detective to his medical examiner to his university expert thought was justified.

And just in case the jury didn't get it, a ruthless, talented, engaging, beautiful defense attorney would make sure they understood too.

Brunelle parked his car in the hotel lot and looked in the direction of the casino. He needed a drink.

~*~

He decided to check in first. His room was fine. Nothing special, but not too bad. He could certainly make himself comfortable here for the next few weeks.

He set his bag on the bed and looked out the window. He had a partially obstructed view of the Tacoma skyline. The city wasn't nearly as big as Seattle, but it was built on a steep incline so even the shorter buildings looked like skyscrapers if they were far enough up the hill. The Tacoma Dome stadium and an art deco bridge were lit up, making the city look inviting, at least from a distance.

He turned away and considered that drink again. He realized he also hadn't had dinner yet and recalled, with some sadness, that Freddy had claimed the casino had the best all-you-could-eat buffet around. So, despite the temptation to find a more cosmopolitan drinking spot downtown, the lure of cheap food and the ability to walk home after having had too much to drink helped the casino win out over some unknown bar in Tacoma proper.

He grabbed his key-card and looked at his phone. Nothing more depressing than a middle-aged man drinking by himself. Maybe Kat wasn't quite as angry any more. Maybe she'd drive down, if he said the right things…

No.

Maybe Talon was around. Maybe they could restart negotiations. See where that unbuttoned blouse might lead to…

No.

He frowned and turned off the light. He closed the door behind him and headed for the casino.

Maybe he'd get lucky.

CHAPTER 30

Laura? No.

Lindsey? No.

Damn.

Brunelle couldn't remember the name of the waitress he was bringing back to his hotel room.

Something with an 'L.' Lisa? No.

He fumbled for his key-card as the woman hung on his shoulder and giggled.

Just don't call her Kat. Or Talon. Or Debra. Or...

The room door popped open and they tumbled inside. Brunelle pushed the door closed with his back and pulled Lexi against him. Her tongue slid into his mouth and his hand slid down the back of her pants.

Bam! Bam! Bam!

"Police! Open the door!"

Brunelle pulled Lucy away and looked at her. She was young, but not that young.

"Open the door now, Mr. Brunelle."

Shit, They know my name? Not good. Probably.

He really wished he weren't drunk.

Lilly stumbled away as Brunelle turned and opened the door. Three police officers stood behind Detective Sixrivers. "Please step out of the room, Mr. Brunelle. You and your lady friend."

Leslie looked to Brunelle. He nodded. "We do what they say."

She stepped quickly around Brunelle and into the hallway. Then she tugged Sixrivers sleeve. "Can I just go? I don't even know his name."

The detective stared at her for a moment, then nodded. She bolted for the lobby, practically leaving a waitress-shaped cloud of smoke behind.

"What's going on?" Brunelle asked Sixrivers.

Sixrivers didn't reply. He just stood there, cross-armed. After a moment, he gave Brunelle the courtesy of a glance and disapproving head-shake. Brunelle shrugged and leaned against the wall. He knew he'd find out soon enough.

A minute later, one of the patrol officers stepped into the hallway.

"The tip was right, detective." He held up Quilcene's ivory-handled knife. "We found it under the bed."

CHAPTER 31

Sixrivers slid the constitutional rights advisement across the table to Brunelle and clicked on the recorder.

"I believe we've done this before," he said.

Brunelle nodded and sighed. "Yes, we have."

"You know I have to read them on the recording," Sixrivers said. "So here we go. You have the right to remain silent..."

Brunelle followed along the form as Sixrivers read each right out loud. When he'd finished, the detective asked the two questions printed at the bottom of the sheet.

"Do you understand each of these rights as I've read them to you?"

"Yes," answered Brunelle.

"Understanding these rights, do you voluntarily wish to answer questions?"

"No way."

Sixrivers' shoulders dropped. "Come on, Brunelle. You know that makes you look guilty."

"Come on, yourself, detective," Brunelle replied. "You know you can't tell the jury I invoked, so it doesn't make me look anything. I do this for a living. I know the best thing anyone can do is remain silent."

Sixrivers stroked his chin. "So you're already thinking about a jury? You expect to get charged?"

Brunelle shook his head at the detective and tapped the rights form, then his own chest. "Right to remain silent. Invoking."

Sixrivers pushed back in his chair. He crossed his arms and gave Brunelle a long appraisal.

"Look, Brunelle," he said. "We both know you didn't steal that knife. You were set up. We got an anonymous tip to check your room. That means it was somebody who knew you'd be down here."

Brunelle nodded, but didn't say anything. *Remain silent,* he reminded himself.

"So, help me out, huh?" Sixrivers went on. "Is there someone who's mad at you right now?"

Kat.

"Someone who might want you out of commission for a while?"

Talon.

Someone who resents you being involved in this case in the first place?"

Quilcene. LeClair. You. Everyone.

Sixrivers gave Brunelle another few moments to say something, anything, then sighed. "Fine. Have it your way."

He clicked off the recorder and stood up. "You're under arrest."

Brunelle looked up at him. "For what?"

"Possession of stolen property and tampering with evidence." He grabbed a hold of Brunelle's arm. Not roughly, but firmly enough to show he meant it. "Stand up and put your hands behind your back.

Brunelle did as he was told. "Is this really necessary?"

"Standard procedure," Sixrivers answered. "I'll take 'em off when we get to the jail."

~*~

Brunelle had thought he'd end up in some holding cell in the basement of the tribal police department. Instead, Sixrivers drove him downtown to the Pierce County Jail.

As they parked and Sixrivers helped Brunelle out of the backseat, the detective said, "Don't worry. I'll tell them you're a prosecutor. They can't put you in general population. If you've got someone you can call to make bail, they may just keep you in booking until it's posted. Then get the hell out of here. For good."

Brunelle nodded. "Right. Thanks."

"You got someone you can call?"

Brunelle sighed. "Yeah. I think so."

~*~

Please answer, please answer, Brunelle thought as he pressed the buttons on what must have been the only pay-phone left on the West Coast.

'Hello. This is Kat Anderson. I'm sorry I missed your call. Please leave a message and I'll call you back.'

Damn.

Beep!

"Hey, Kat. It's David. Um, you're not going to believe this…"

~*~

An hour later, Brunelle was still in booking when his holding cell door clanked open.

"Your bail just got posted," the burly guard informed him. "You can go."

Thank God, Brunelle thought. *And thank you, Kat.*

He fetched his belt and shoes from the locker they'd been stashed inside and hurried out to the lobby. Despite everything, he couldn't suppress a smile. Kat still cared enough to bail him out.

But when he got to to the lobby, he found Chen standing there.

"Oh. It's just you."

"Wow," Chen replied. "Nice to see you too. Did they mention that it was 'just me' who just bailed your ass out of jail?"

Brunelle nodded and finished fastening his belt. "Sorry. Yes. Thank you. I was just hoping…"

"It would have been Kat?" Chen finished.

Brunelle shrugged. "Yeah."

Chen put an arm around his friend's shoulder. "Well, cheer up. She was the one who called me."

"Yeah?" Brunelle looked over at Chen.

"Yeah," Chen answered. "She's too good for you. You know that, right?"

Brunelle looked down again. "Yeah, I know that. Thanks, buddy."

Chen pulled his arm back. "No worries. Now, let's get you back to your hotel. You've got a murder trial to start tomorrow. And I've got an investigation to start."

"Another murder?" Brunelle asked.

Chen smiled. "No. Planting evidence. You worry about convicting Quilcene. I'll figure out who did this to you."

CHAPTER 32

"Are the parties ready in the matter of the Puyallup Indian Tribe versus John Quilcene?"

Judge LeClair looked down from the bench, awaiting the lawyers' replies. So too did the full gallery and three television cameras. Local, national, and cable. A murder trial in a Native tribal court was big news.

Brunelle stood. "The prosecution is ready, Your Honor."

"The defense is ready," Talon answered as she too stood up. She was wearing a black power suit with a blood red silk blouse. It matched Brunelle's black suit and red power tie perfectly. It just reminded him that they could have been a great team, under different circumstances.

"It is my understanding," the judge said carefully, "that there may be an issue regarding a particular piece of evidence?"

Brunelle winced. He should have realized news would travel fast.

"Er, yes," he started, but Talon interrupted.

"I'm aware of the situation, Your Honor," she said, "and we will stipulate to chain of custody and to the admissibility of the knife collected—" She paused to throw a playful glance at Brunelle. "—*originally* collected at the scene of the killing here."

Judge LeClair raised his eyebrows.

Brunelle was a bit surprised as well. "Uh...," he stammered.

The judge saved him. "Any objection to that stipulation, Mr. Brunelle?"

He stood speechless for a moment, trying to figure out why she would be doing this for him. "Uh, no, Your Honor. No objection."

LeClair exhaled. "Good." He looked at the gallery, the cameras, then back to the lawyers. "Now, let's discuss scheduling."

Brunelle and Talon both nodded, but remained silent.

"We will select the jury this morning," the judge declared. "Mr. Brunelle will you be prepared to give your opening statement after lunch?"

Brunelle would have preferred waiting until the next morning for openings. A night of drinking, frustrated romantic intentions, and being arrested wasn't the best preparation for the killer opening he knew he needed to give.

"Yes, Your Honor," he replied. "Absolutely."

LeClair turned to Talon. "Ms. Winter, will you be giving your opening statement after Mr. Brunelle's, or are you going to reserve until the close of the prosecution's evidence?"

"Oh, no. I'll be delivering my opening statement immediately after the prosecution. There's no way I'm going to let the jury hear all of the prosecution's evidence without understanding what this case is really about."

Wonderful, thought Brunelle, trying not to roll his eyes.

"All right then," LeClair said. "Mr. Brunelle, plan to have at least one witness available after lunch. Assuming you two lawyers don't use up the entire afternoon talking, I'd like to get right into testimony."

"Yes, Your Honor," Brunelle answered. He already had Chen lined up. Usually, he preferred to lead with a member of the victim's family. Someone to humanize the victim. But Traver didn't have any family, and Brunelle knew he wasn't going to win by pretending Traver was anything other than the scumbag he was. He was going to win despite it.

"Court will be at recess for fifteen minutes," Judge LeClair announced. "When I return, we will begin jury selection."

"All rise!" ordered the bailiff.

Once the judge left the bench, Brunelle stepped over to Talon.

"Thanks for stipulating to the knife," he whispered, one eye on the cameras. "That could have been a little embarrassing."

Talon smiled broadly. "No problem, Dave. I don't want you embarrassed by that."

Brunelle returned the smile.

"I want to you to be embarrassed when I kick your ass."

Brunelle looked down and shook his head at the repeated taunt.

"Oh, don't look so pouty, Dave," Talon chirped. "Be glad I need you or I would have let you get kicked off this case long ago."

He looked up. "Need me?"

"Of course." That predator's smile again. "I told you: I'm going to make a name for myself with this case. I'm going to use you. That's what lawyers do, right? We use people."

Brunelle smiled weakly. "Yeah. I've heard that."

~*~

Jury selection was mundane. Brunelle had already decided that as the outsider, with the entire jury pool being drawn from the tribal rolls, he wasn't going to stand up and strike any potential jurors unless they were absolutely unacceptable. Luckily, everyone seemed normal enough, interested without being overly so, and promised to keep an open mind.

Talon used all six of her preemptory challenges on women, resulting, when the dust settled, in a jury of ten men and two women.

When they broke for lunch, Brunelle pulled her aside. "You know it's unethical to strike potential jurors just because of their race or gender."

Talon stared at him for a moment. "Then you should have objected."

Brunelle shrugged. "I don't mind. You do what you think you need to do. I would have thought you'd want women on the jury, especially mothers, given what Traver did."

Talon grinned. "Mothers would have wanted to kill that bastard," she agreed. "But the fathers actually would have done it."

Brunelle tried to keep a poker face. *Damn good point*, he thought.

"Besides," Talon smoothed her suit against her athletic body. "Remember how close I got you to giving me that manslaughter? Well, I'm going to use every weapon I have to kick—"

"My ass," he finished for her. "Got it."

"Good," Talon laughed. "But don't worry. I'll keep reminding you."

CHAPTER 33

"Ladies and gentlemen of the jury," Judge LeClair announced when court reconvened, "please give your attention to Mr. Brunelle, who will deliver the opening statement on behalf of the prosecution."

Brunelle stood up and thanked the judge. He straightened his jacket and glanced at the gallery. In addition to the defendant's family and all the media, Duncan had driven down for the openings. Sixrivers was there too, standing in the back, arms crossed. Even long-time rival Jessica Edwards from the King County public defender's office had shown up. Everyone wanted to see how ol' Dave would do with this one.

No pressure.

He pulled together his serious expression and looked at the jury.

"George Traver," he began, pausing long enough to let people anticipate his next words, "was a miserable bastard who deserved to die."

Confusion passed over the faces of the jurors almost as quickly as the murmur of astonishment rippled through the gallery.

"He was a child molester. The worst kind of scum. Even in prison they have to house the child molesters away from the rest of the criminals, just for their own safety. Traver preyed on defenseless children, taking advantage of their trusting nature, and destroying their innocence.

"If the defendant, Mr. John Quilcene, hadn't killed him, then there is absolutely no doubt that George Traver would have molested another child, stolen another young girl's innocence, destroyed another life."

Then, just so everyone understood his point, he added, "The world is a better place now that George Traver is dead."

Brunelle allowed himself a moment to pace a few steps and survey the courtroom. In part, to let his words sink in with the jury. In part, to catch a glimpse of the flabbergasted expression plastered on Talon's exquisite face.

"Now, let me step back a moment," he continued, "and explain that this is opening statement. It is *not* evidence. It is simply a summary of what I expect the evidence will show. Evidence is what the witnesses say. It's the photographs and diagrams and exhibits admitted during the trial. I'm just a lawyer. So is Ms. Winter. We present the evidence, but we don't create it. If a lawyer tells you anything in opening statement that is not supported by the evidence, then you must disregard what the lawyer says entirely.

"Another important thing is that this is opening *statement*, not, as it's sometimes called on TV, opening *argument*. A trial starts with opening statements, and ends with closing arguments. Right now, I'm going to tell you what happened. I am not going to tell you what your verdict should be. That would be argument and that is reserved for the end of the trial—after you've heard all the evidence and the judge tells you what the law actually is. Only then would it be fair to argue what your verdict should be. If I argued that now,

Ms. Winter would object and she would be right to do so. And the judge would sustain the objection, and he would be right to do so.

"So no arguments. Just the facts. Just the story of what happened. And here is that story."

Another pause to refocus everyone's attention after the dry, but strategic, treatise on openings versus closings. Then he launched into it.

"George Traver was a child molester. He'd been convicted twice and spent several years in prison. When he got out he was required to register as a sex offender. He was supposed to check in with the police and provide his current address. If he moved, he had to update it. And if he became homeless, he had to appear personally every week to make sure he was still around.

"Unfortunately, the reason for all this is that child molesters tend to reoffend. I won't bore you with the details, but treatment is rarely successful for people who like to do what George Traver liked to do. Registration is supposed to help against that by letting police and neighbors know when a pedophile moves into the neighborhood. If they can't stop themselves, at least we can watch our kids a little closer.

"But the system breaks down when the pedophile decides not to register any more and just disappears. That's a crime in itself—Failing to Register as a Sex Offender. Well, as you might have guessed, George Traver decided he didn't want to register any more. And a warrant was issued for his arrest."

Brunelle assessed the jury. He had them. The beauty of always going first was that the jury hadn't heard the story yet, but they were dying to know. They could guess bits and pieces from the questions the lawyers asked during jury selection. The judge told them the name of the crime charged. Maybe they'd seen something in the news. But they didn't know the details. The juicy, horrible details. And Brunelle got first crack at telling them.

"Now, this story should have had a happy ending," he continued. "I should be able to tell you that George Traver made his way up to Seattle where he was identified and detained by a Seattle Police detective. I should be able to tell you that this detective ran Traver for warrants and found, not just the warrant for failing to register, but two more for theft and drinking in public. I should be able to tell you that this detective arrested George Traver, that Traver was charged with failing to register, and that he was convicted and sent back to prison, where his sick, child-molesting self deserved to be—far, far away from our children."

Brunelle set his jaw. "But I can't tell you that.

"Because that detective did encounter Traver, did identify him, did run him for warrants, and did see, not one, but three active warrants."

A pause.

"And then that detective let Traver go."

There were gasps in the gallery. The jurors knew better than to gasp themselves, but their eyes held the same disbelief.

"Instead, he told Traver he'd look the other way if Traver would work as an informant, snitching on gang activity in downtown Seattle. Specifically, the activity of the Native Gangster Bloods, a Native American gang centered right here in the Puyallup tribe."

Brunelle took a moment to survey the room. The shock on Talon's face had been replaced with thinly veiled anger. Or at least frustration.

Brunelle smiled to himself. Three steps ahead isn't good if your opponent takes an unexpected fork in the road behind you.

"And that's why George Traver was not in prison on the day he decided to rape three-year-old Caitlyn Quilcene."

This time the gasp—fueled by anger and revulsion— extended to some of the jurors.

"Three-year-old Caitlyn Quilcene," Brunelle repeated. "The defendant's niece. Traver destroyed that little girl's life. He didn't murder her, but her killed her innocence. He slaughtered the childhood she should have had, and in that way, George Traver was a murderer too."

Brunelle paused again. He was experienced enough not to do the rookie pacing in front of the jury box, but he did move as he delivered an opening, aware of his positioning at all times. He stopped directly in front of the middle of the jury box. He borrowed the affect of O'Brien the professor, resting an elbow on one hand while tapping his lips.

"There is a tradition in Native American law," he chose the phrase carefully, "called blood revenge. If someone in your tribe were killed, then you had the right and the duty to kill someone in the killer's tribe. And the members of that clan would have a duty to accept the revenge killing.

"In this case, Mr. Quilcene had a ceremonial knife. You'll see it. It has an intricately carved ivory handle. Mr. Quilcene took that knife and he went up to Seattle to find George Traver. And when he found him, he confronted him. And then he killed him.

"He stabbed him in the stomach and in the chest. The blow to the stomach would have disabled him. The blow to the chest went directly into Traver's heart, instantly killing that miserable, child-molesting bastard. Then, Mr. Quilcene left the knife in Traver's chest and walked calmly, and righteously, away."

Brunelle straightened his jacket again, looking down for a moment. The silences were as important as the words. He looked up at the jurors again.

"That's what happened, ladies and gentlemen. And at the

end of the trial I'll stand up again and explain to you why—despite everything you're feeling right now—that's murder in the first degree. Thank you."

Brunelle sat down and made sure not to look directly at Talon. Too many people were watching. But even though he couldn't see her face, he got his satisfaction after the judge said, "Now, ladies and gentlemen, please give your attention to Ms. Winter, who will give opening statement on behalf of the defendant."

Talon stood up just long enough to say, "The defense will reserve opening statement, Your Honor."

Brunelle suppressed a begrudging smile. He was impressed. He'd learned a long time ago, that while it was good to win on your facts, it was even better to win on theirs. His plan was to give Talon's opening, then object like crazy if she started to argue her justifiable homicide theory. It was opening statement, not closing argument. She could say what happened, but not why it was okay. The judge should sustain his objections. He wasn't sure if he would, but he should.

And apparently, Talon thought so too.

It took LeClair a moment to recover from Talon's unexpected announcement. There was a reasons he had asked her in advance if she was going to reserve. He didn't want to look like a jackass in front of the jury. Now he did, thanks to Talon. Bonus for Brunelle.

"All right then," the judge regained himself. "Mr. Brunelle, is the prosecution ready to call its first witness?"

"Yes, Your Honor," Brunelle stood up. "The prosecution calls Detective Lawrence Chen."

CHAPTER 34

Chen turned out to be a spectacularly uninteresting witness. He identified himself. He recited his rank and duties. He described being called out to the scene and arriving after patrol officers had already cordoned off the area. He moved on to the arrest of Quilcene and finished with the mostly fruitless interrogation of Quilcene.

Brunelle knew he had to be careful when it came to what Quilcene said. He couldn't touch any time Quilcene refused to answer a question, since telling the jury about it would have violated Quilcene's right to remain silent. So he had to be surgical. One carefully rehearsed question and answer.

"What did Mr. Quilcene say regarding the murder of George Traver?"

Chen looked over at the jury to give his answer. "He said, 'The fucker deserved it.'"

"Thank you." Brunelle looked up to the judge. "No further questions, Your Honor."

Judge LeClair looked to Talon. "Any cross examination?"

"Yes, Your Honor." Talon stood up. "Thank you."

She stepped out from behind counsel table. It was the first time the gallery—and all the male jurors—got a good look of her in action.

"So, Detective Chen." She walked right up to the witness stand. "Did the fucker deserve it?"

"Objection!" Brunelle stood up.

Talon looked innocently at the judge. "What's the basis of the objection, Your Honor?"

LeClair glared down at Brunelle. "Basis?"

Brunelle rolled his eyes mentally. It seemed so obviously objectionable, but now he needed to pull the applicable rule out of his memory. "Well, for starters, it calls for a legal conclusion."

That was the right basis.

The judge overruled it anyway. He looked at Chen. "You may answer the question, if you can."

Chen squirmed in the witness chair. "What was the question again?"

Talon smiled, only too eager to get to repeat her question for the jury. "I asked, 'Did the fucker deserve it?'"

Chen took a deep breath and looked to Brunelle for guidance. Brunelle just shrugged and nodded for him to answer the question.

Chen looked back at Talon. "That's not for me to say, ma'am."

"Okay. Fine." Talon nodded. "You have cases, don't you, detective, where it's absolutely clear that the victim in no way deserved what happened to them?"

Chen mouth twisted into a tight knot. "Yes, ma'am," he admitted.

"This isn't one of these cases, is it, detective?"

Chen looked down. "No, ma'am."

Talon nodded. "No further questions."

And thus ended the first day of trial.

CHAPTER 35

Chen had tried to apologize after his testimony but Brunelle had refused to accept it. The case was the case. He wasn't going to fool the jury into thinking Traver was some kind of saint. In truth, Chen had helped the cause. At least the jury knew Brunelle was honest in his opening.

The next witness would be far more important: Kat.

Brunelle had told the jury that the stab to the heart was a premeditated revenge killing. He hadn't used those exact words, but it was the only conclusion from the words he had used. And he would label it accordingly in his closing. But first he had to explain to the jury exactly how Traver died and—since Quilcene never actually admitted to the murder—why a blow to the heart could be enough to infer the premeditated intent he needed for a first degree murder conviction. Kat would be key to that.

Too bad he didn't trust what she might say on the stand. They'd had a great rapport their last trial together. Now, Brunelle wasn't completely convinced she'd even show up the next morning.

He stepped out onto his hotel room balcony and regarded the Tacoma skyline, its reflection twinkling in the water. He took out his cell phone and dialed Kat's number. He told himself it was standard procedure to confirm the next day's witnesses. He couldn't help it if that meant he'd have to combine work with pleasure. Well, maybe not pleasure, but personal business, anyway. He wasn't at all sure it would be pleasurable if she actually answered.

But it turned out he didn't need to worry about that. His call went straight to voicemail.

"Hey, Kat. It's David. Just calling to confirm you're still coming to testify first thing tomorrow morning." He paused. "Well, not just that. I'm also calling to apologize. Again. And to explain. I really didn't set you up at dinner. I had no idea O'Brien would be there and— Aw, crap. Never mind. I'm not going to fill up your voicemail with this. Maybe just give me a call tonight if you can. I'd like to talk to you. Um, okay. Thanks. Bye."

He held the phone to his forehead for several seconds.

Damn.

Why did he care so much?

He'd wanted to suggest they grab dinner again. That night. Use talking over the case as an excuse to be together. But that wasn't going to happen. Still, he needed to eat. With a shrug he grabbed his key-card and his wallet. After the disaster of the previous night, he decided to avoid the casino. Take-out and dinner in the hotel room would be just fine.

~*~

A half hour later, Brunelle was sitting on his bed, a binder of reports on his lap and a half-eaten pizza in the greasy box next to him.

His cell phone rang. He snatched it off the bedside table and looked at the display.

It wasn't Kat. It was Chen.

"Hello?" he answered, not even trying to hide his

disappointment.

"Whatcha doing?" Chen asked.

Brunelle appraised himself for a moment. "Looking at autopsy photographs while eating pizza. Man, this job warps you. Why? What's up?"

"Turn on the TV."

That didn't sound good. He grabbed the remote and clicked on the set directly in front of his bed. "What channel?"

"Local news," Chen answered. "Any of them."

Brunelle surfed to the the single digits and dropped the remote. "Oh, shit."

"Yeah," Chen agreed.

The tagline at the bottom of the screen read, 'Gang Shooting in Tacoma,' but Brunelle recognized the casino in the background. He stood up and looked out the window. He could see the cop cars' lights flashing across the freeway.

"Is it related?" he asked.

"I checked with my contacts at Tacoma P.D.," Chen answered. "They said the victim is NGB."

"Tell me it's not another one of Quilcene's cousins."

"Okay, I won't tell you."

Brunelle's heart dropped. "Fuck. Really?"

"No, actually," Chen said. "But my guy says it's a known associate of Quilcene's. I don't know yet how close they are. I'm about to drive down there. Want me to pick you up?"

Brunelle gazed across at the casino again, then looked at his cadaver-filled binders. He already knew the autopsy report by heart. "Yeah, come get me."

Then he went ahead and asked the most important question.

"Are we going to the morgue or the hospital?"

"Hospital," Chen answered. "He's not dead yet."

Brunelle relaxed a bit. "Well, that's good."

"I said 'yet'," Chen reminded him.

Brunelle considered the Traver-to-Cousin-to-Freddy-to-Associate pattern, and who would be next on the list if this particular NGB died.

"Thank Heaven for small mercies," he said. "Call me when you get here."

CHAPTER 36

Tacoma General Hospital was located at the top of Tacoma's downtown, right next to the Hilltop neighborhood and across the street from Wright Park, the largest city park in the U.S. after New York's Central Park. But Tacoma was a lot smaller than New York and Chen had no trouble finding on-street parking right by the entrance to the emergency room. It was starting to rain heavily, so both men turned up their collars and hurried into the hospital's lobby.

"Do you know what room he's in?" Brunelle asked, scanning the lobby for a directory.

"Chen pulled out his phone and checked his text messages. "214-C. Intensive care."

Brunelle frowned. "Damn."

Chen let out a small laugh and patted his friend on the shoulder. "Yeah. Well, for once, let's hope a gang-banger pulls through.

Upstairs they found the ICU and room 214-C. There was a large 'No Admittance' sign on the door, plus two cops standing outside. Chen's Tacoma P.D. connection. And Sixrivers.

"Hey, Paul," Chen greeted the Tacoma officer. Then the introductions. "Paul, this is Dave Brunelle from the King County Prosecutor's Office. Dave, this is Paul Mulholland, Tacoma detective."

Brunelle and Mulholland shook hands. "Nice to meet you," said Brunelle. Then he nodded to Sixrivers. "Always good to see you too, detective."

Sixrivers smiled at that. "Well, maybe not always, huh?" Then he answered the obvious question. "I'm here because it happened on tribal land. But honestly, we're not equipped for all this violence. So we called in Tacoma."

"So what's the story?" Brunelle deflected the conversation. "Who is this guy?"

"His name is Sam Hernandez," Mulholland reported.

"Hernandez?" Brunelle questioned. "I thought he was NGB."

"We're not all named 'Dances with Wolves,'" Sixrivers intoned.

Brunelle nodded sheepishly.

"What he wants to know," Chen clarified, "is how this guy is related to Johnny Quilcene?"

"Best friend," Sixrivers answered. "They grew up together, got jumped into the gang at the same time, the whole bit."

Brunelle shook his head. *Not good.* "What's his condition?"

"Critical," Mulholland answered. "He took three rounds to the chest. Missed his heart, but took out a lung and he's lost a lot of blood. Basically, he's on life support. They don't think he's going to make it."

Brunelle frowned as he confirmed the timeline in his head. "Quilcene was out on bail when Freddy got shot, wasn't he?"

Sixrivers nodded. "Yep. And he's still out."

"Who's Freddy?" Mulholland asked.

"He's the one who took up Traver's blood feud," Brunelle said darkly.

Mulholland's face twisted into a puzzled expression. "What the hell does that mean?"

"It means," Chen said, putting a hand on Brunelle's shoulder, "call me immediately if Hernandez dies."

CHAPTER 37

The next morning Brunelle almost would have been willing to trade places with Sam Hernandez. He had ex-girlfriends, and he'd had to call hostile witnesses, but he'd never had to call a hostile ex-girlfriend as a witness. Especially a hostile ex-girlfriend who'd never quite made it to girlfriend status in the first place, which was probably why she was so hostile.

Once everyone had assembled for the resumption of trial, Judge LeClair looked down at Brunelle and said, "The prosecution may call its next witness."

"The prosecution calls Dr. Kat Anderson."

Here goes nothing.

Brunelle went to the hallway and stuck his head out. "Okay, Kat. You're up."

Kat set down her paperback and picked up her case file. She stood up and walked into the courtroom. All without meeting Brunelle's gaze.

"You look lovely today, doctor," Brunelle whispered as she passed him, but she ignored him and marched to the witness stand to be sworn in.

Brunelle sighed, then gathered himself and stepped into the attorney well between the jury box, the witness stand and the bench. He straightened his exhibits on the bar—autopsy photos, written reports, diagrams of the wounds—and began.

"Please state your name for the record."

"Kat Anderson."

"And how are you employed, ma'am?"

"I am an assistant medical examiner with the King County Medical Examiner's Office."

So far so good. Kat was cold, but she was answering his questions, turning to the jury to deliver her answers like she was supposed to do. And she wasn't sneering at him. They might never get together after all, but he was starting to think he would survive the direct examination.

"How long have you been an assistant medical examiner?"

"Almost nine years."

"Did you have any medical training prior to that?"

"Yes. I worked as a resident at Tacoma General Hospital," she told the jury with a sweet smile. Then she turned to back to Brunelle. "I believe we've previously discussed my time there. Or have you forgotten again?"

Brunelle's heart skipped a beat. He certainly remembered their conversations: about how she'd dated Freddy while she was a resident there, and how he'd forgotten to tell her he'd been murdered.

She was toying with him.

He wanted to trust her. But he didn't.

"Your Honor." Brunelle looked up to Judge LeClair, his eyes a bit too wide. "May we discuss a matter outside the presence of the jury?"

He was going to ask that Kat be declared a hostile witness.

Then he could ask her leading questions and control her responses.

The judge offered a quizzical expression. "You just started, Mr. Brunelle."

Kat gave the slightest eye roll, almost imperceptible. He looked at her. She crossed her arms. "Really?" she asked quietly.

Brunelle looked back to the judge. "Er, right. Sorry." *Damn her for flustering me so easily.* "I think it can wait after all. My apoligies."

Judge LeClair lowered his eyebrows at Brunelle. "Good. You may proceed, counselor."

I may, thought Brunelle. *But do I dare?*

"Yes, well..." He gathered his wits again. "Is it one of your duties to conduct autopsies, Dr. Anderson?"

Kat nodded and turned to the jury. "I would say," she told them, "that's my main duty."

"And what is the purpose of an autopsy?"

"The primary purpose of an autopsy is to determine the manner of death."

"Okay, great." Brunelle could feel his heart slowing. "Let's unpack that answer a bit."

Kat winced at the cliché, but nodded and waited for the rest of the question.

"You said the primary purpose is to determine the manner of death," Brunelle repeated. "Are there other purposes?"

"Yes." Kat turned again to the jury, delivering her answer like a teacher delivering a lesson. "There may be other physical evidence—injuries or toxicology—which, while not directly contributing to the subject's death, may nevertheless shed light for the investigators on how the death may have occurred."

"So are you involved in trying to recreate exactly what happened at the time the person was killed?"

"No, that's for the detectives," Kat answered. "As I said, I determine the manner of death. The detectives determine what happened."

Brunelle nodded. "What are the possible manners of death?" he continued.

"There are four." She held up four fingers to the jury and counted them off. "Natural causes, accident, suicide, and homicide."

"Thank you," Brunelle said. Then he picked up his exhibits and handed them to Kat. She took them without looking at him.

"For the record, I've just handed you several documents," Brunelle stated. "Could you identify them, please?"

Kat thumbed through the papers, then looked up. "This is my autopsy report regarding subject George Traver, and these are some of the photographs that were taken during the autopsy."

"Do you recall that autopsy?"

Kat actually bothered to flip through her written report, before answering, "Yes."

"And did you determine a manner of death?"

"Yes," she finally smiled at him. But it was a challenging, 'Remember what I said at the scene?' kind of smile. "Yes, I did."

Brunelle swallowed. *Don't say suicide.* "What was the manner of George Traver's death?"

She paused, then turned to the jury. The poor jury, like children stuck watching a poorly concealed fight between their parents. "George Traver's death was a homicide."

Whew.

That was a huge check mark on his list of information he needed to get to the jury. It was obvious, but he still needed a witness to say it out loud.

Under different circumstances, Brunelle might have tried to draw out the M.E.'s testimony. Really spend some time on all of the wounds. Flash disturbing photographs up on the wall and have the M.E. explain in excruciating detail how a particular wound would cause death, hopefully with some severe suffering. But as it was—with an unsympathetic victim and a witness who hated his guts—he decided to just hit the high points and sit the hell down.

"What major wounds did you identify that led to Traver's death?"

Kat cocked her head at the question. She'd testified hundreds of times. Different prosecutors, but the script was always the same. They were at the place where she described the steps of an autopsy generally, before moving to the specifics of the autopsy in question. Brunelle was going off script. Hurry up offense.

"Uh, the major wounds were two sharp force trauma to the anterior torso. One to the abdomen, the other to the anterior chest which perforated the left ventricle."

"Stab wounds to the stomach and chest," Brunelle translated. "The one to the chest punctured his heart."

Kat grimaced. "Roughly," she admitted.

"The stab wound to his stomach," Brunelle pressed on, "would that have been fatal?"

Kat turned again to the jury. "It could have been, without prompt medical attention. It lacerated his colon, so waste spilled into his abdominal cavity. In addition to bleeding to death internally, there was a great risk of infection."

"But if he'd gotten to a hospital quickly, he could have been saved?"

Kat considered, then nodded. "I believe so, yes."

"But not the stab wound to the heart." It was more statement than question. Definitely leading and therefore objectionable, but Talon was proving what a good litigator she was. Just because you can object, doesn't mean you should. Especially if you want the jury to hear the answer.

"Correct," Kat agreed. "The injury to the heart was instantly fatal. It was not a survivable injury."

Brunelle considered sitting down at the point, but there was one more area he wanted the jury to know about.

"Doctor, could you please explain," he asked, "what is meant by the term 'defensive wounds?'"

Kat nodded and turned to the jury box. "Defensive wounds are injuries which indicate that the victim attempted to defend himself or herself from the assault. They are usually on the hands and arms, often from grabbing the blade or attempting to shield themselves."

Almost done.

"Were there any defensive wounds on Mr. Traver?"

Kat considered for a moment, then reached for report. She turned through several pages, then looked up. "No. There were no defensive wounds on Mr. Traver's hands or arms."

Brunelle exhaled. *Pulled it off.*

"No further questions," he was relieved to say.

The judge looked to Talon as Brunelle sat down. "Ms. Winter? Any cross examination?"

"Yes, Your Honor." Talon stood up. "Thank you."

She stepped toward Kat, but stopped short of the usual, in-your-face distance defense attorneys often took with when conducting a rigorous cross-examination. Instead, her location and affect suggested a friendly rapport.

"Just three areas, doctor," Talon began. "And then I'll sit down."

Kat nodded, a curious smile pushing out onto her lips. "All right."

Brunelle could see Kat was appraising Talon for his

description of 'hottie.' Unfortunately for him, Talon's perfectly tailored suit and patterned leggings just confirmed it.

"First," Talon said. "You testified that Mr. Traver's death was a homicide, correct?"

"Correct."

"Homicide is different from murder, isn't it?"

Kat smiled.

Damn it, she smiled.

Then she turned to the jury. "Absolutely," Kat said. "'Homicide' simply means that the person was killed by another person rather than by some other means. For example, by his own hand—which would be suicide—or accident, or natural causes. But 'murder' is a legal term. It denotes that the homicide was unlawful. I don't make that determination."

"Who does?"

Another smile at the jurors. "The jury."

"And so," Talon confirmed, "it's possible to have a homicide which is not a murder."

One more smile. "Absolutely."

Wow, Brunelle thought as he pretended to be taking notes. *She really does hate me.*

Talon paused, allowing the response to linger in the air.

"Okay, second thing," she said. "You deal with physical injuries, and in particular, physical injuries that cause death, correct?"

Kat frowned in consideration. "Yes, that's correct."

"And physical injuries that cause death, those never heal, do they?"

Kat thought for a moment. "I suppose that's true, with the possible exception of a serious, but initially survivable injury that begins to heal before the person eventually succumbs to it. But yes, generally speaking, a fatal wound, by definition, ceases all of the body's functions, including healing."

Talon nodded. "There are emotional wounds that never heal either, aren't there, doctor?"

"Objection." Brunelle said before he could stop himself. He rarely objected because objecting was like turning to the jury and screaming, 'Ouch! This really hurts my case.' But the question was so outrageous—and unexpected—he just reacted.

"Objection overruled," Judge LeClair without even asking for a response from Talon. "You may answer," he told Kat.

Kat turned and stared right into Brunelle's eyes. "Yes. Yes, there are."

Talon pushed her hair over her shoulder and moved in for the kill. Brunelle could see it in her eyes. And they both knew he wasn't going to object again.

"And finally, Dr. Anderson, you know what George Traver did to my client's niece, don't you?"

Kat nodded. "Yes, I know."

"You have a daughter, don't you, doctor?"

Fuck. How does she know that?...Three steps ahead.

"Yes," Kat took a moment to reply. "Yes, I do."

"Can you blame Johnny for what he did?"

Kat sat silently for a several seconds. She looked down and her mouth screwed into a knot. Without looking up, she answered. "No. No, I can't."

Talon waited for a moment, nodding at the response she'd elicited. "Thank you for your candor, doctor. No further questions."

The judge waited a few more seconds before asking, "Any re-direct, Mr. Brunelle?"

No fucking way. "No, Your Honor."

"You are excused," Judge LeClair told Kat. Then he

addressed the jury. "Ladies and gentlemen, we will take a fifteen minute recess before the next witness."

Brunelle was glad for the break, but he knew it wasn't going to get any better. After Kat stormed out without a word to him and the jury closed the jury room door behind them, Talon stepped over.

"Who's next?" she asked.

Brunelle grimaced. "Caitlyn's mom."

CHAPTER 38

"The prosecution calls Stacy Quilcene."

All eyes turned to the doorway. Brunelle pushed it open to gesture for the mother of Traver's victim to enter the courtroom. She had dressed up in a blouse and skirt—the kind of thing someone might wear to church or a job interview. But there was no mistaking it, she was a mother. The only reason she hadn't killed Traver is that her brother did it first.

Unfortunately, Brunelle needed to call her in his case, but it was a calculated risk. She would prove the motive. But, his opening statement notwithstanding, the last thing he wanted was for her to connect with the jury. They were already going to feel inclined to walk Quilcene based on what he had done. He didn't need them to feel like they owed an acquittal to Stacy—or Caitlyn.

So it would be fast.

"Please state your name for the record."

"Stacy Quilcene."

"How are you related to the defendant?"

"He's my brother."

"Do you have a daughter named Caitlyn?"

"Yes. I have three kids. Caitlyn's my baby."

Great. The baby. If he hadn't been sure of his course of action before, he was then.

"Caitlyn was molested, right?"

The question was so brash, so matter-of-fact, it stunned Stacy for a moment. "Er, yes. That's correct."

"And the man who molested her, that was George Traver?"

Stacy narrowed her momma-bear eyes and replied through gritted teeth. "Yes. George Traver molested my little baby girl."

Technically, Stacy's knowledge of what happened to her daughter was hearsay. She wasn't present for it; she couldn't have been—she never would have allowed it. So whatever she knew about it, she learned from other people, like Caitlyn. Hearsay was usually inadmissible, but there were too many exceptions to count, including a very specific statute on statements made by child victims of sexual assault. One way or another, the story was coming in. But he didn't want details. He wanted motive.

"Did you tell your brother what Traver did to Caitlyn?"

"Damn right I did."

"And what did he do?"

"He killed that mother fucker."

Brunelle nodded. "Thank you. Ms. Quilcene. No further questions."

Talon stood up. This was the dangerous part. Brunelle had avoided details, but he knew Talon wanted them out and to the jury. He'd kept his direct short enough that he might be able to object to details as 'beyond the scope' of his questions. But Judge LeClair hadn't helped him on any of his objections so far, and anyway, what few questions he did ask—specifically the fact that Caitlyn had in fact been molested—probably opened the door to Talon going into the heart-wrenching details.

So Brunelle was stunned, and delighted, when Talon announced, "No questions, Your Honor."

But his delight evaporated when she went on to explain, "We'll be calling Ms. Quilcene in our case-in-chief."

Damn.

Brunelle hated it when defendants actually put on a case. More often than not, they just sat there, hiding behind the burden of proof. But he should have known Talon would do the best thing possible: tell her story, through her own witnesses, when it was her turn. Not piecemeal on cross-examination in the middle of his case.

The only good news was that it let Brunelle present his case interrupted. He just had to hope that by the time Talon got around to putting on her evidence, the jury would already be leaning his way.

Which made O'Brien's testimony critical.

CHAPTER 39

O'Brien went full professor for his testimony. Brunelle wished he hadn't. Khakis, cream turtleneck, and tweed jacket. With patches on the elbows, of course. And the glasses. Add in the swept back curls and he was ready to give a lecture to a hundred college kids.

Brunelle knew the jury hated him already.

"William O'Brien," he replied to the standard first question of identifying himself. "Ph.D."

Adding his degree wasn't going to help.

"How are you employed, sir?" Brunelle asked next. He decided not to call him 'doctor.'

"I am a professor of Native American studies at the University of Washington."

That sentence, in that tone, in that court, with those jurors and that gallery, made O'Brien look even whiter than Brunelle.

Brunelle pressed on, drawing out O'Brien's credentials: his years of teaching experience, his awards and published articles, and his general expertise on things Native American. Then he got to the meat of the matter.

"Are you familiar with a cultural phenomenon known as 'blood revenge'?"

The question seemed to wake the jury up again after the nap-inducing recitation of degrees and recognitions.

"Yes," O'Brien answered. "I am very familiar with the tradition of blood revenge."

And here we go.

"Could you please tell the jury what blood revenge is?"

"Well," O'Brien turned slightly toward the jury but also tried to look at Brunelle. He obviously hadn't testified much. "The first thing to understand is that the notion of blood revenge is not unique to Native American culture. Indeed, there is no such thing as a single Native American culture. There are hundreds of nations and tribes all over North and South America, each with their own—"

"Professor?" Brunelle interrupted.

"Yes?" O'Brien was a bit taken aback by the interruption. Brunelle guessed his lectures seldom included question and answer sessions.

"We'll get to all that," Brunelle said. "But first, can you please just tell the jury what blood revenge is? Then we can discuss its significance and prevalence."

"Ah, yes." O'Brien nodded. "Right. Sorry."

He turned fully to the jury this time. "Blood revenge is the killing of one tribe or family member in retaliation for the death of someone in one's own tribe at the hands of a member of the offending tribe."

"Is this sort of killing supposed to settle the score then?" Brunelle explained for the jurors.

"If accepted by both tribes, then yes, the blood revenge killing will balance the scales and life as normal may proceed."

Brunelle nodded. *Stage one complete. On to stage two.*

"So what is a blood *feud*?" he asked.

O'Brien thought for a moment. "A blood feud is what happens when the blood revenge killing is not accepted by the tribe against whom the revenge is targeted. They do not accept it as a settling of the score and follow up with a blood revenge killing of their own. This can lead to a potentially endless cycle of retaliation and killing. In fact," he took off his glasses, "it was exactly this sort of out of control blood feuding which likely led to the Iroquois Confederacy in the Northeast—"

"Okay, thank you, professor," Brunelle interrupted again. "Let's try to keep things local."

O'Brien forced a smile. He was obviously used to getting to speak uninterrupted. "All right then."

"Are you familiar with the custom of Northwest tribes regarding blood revenge?"

"Yes," O'Brien replied. "I received my doctorate from the University of Iowa, and so my dissertation was on marriage customs in agrarian Plains tribes, but I am familiar with most cultural aspects of most Native tribes."

Great.

"Okay," Brunelle pressed on quickly. He checked Talon out of the corner of his eye, in case she might try to challenge O'Brien's qualifications. But she was just listening and taking notes. When she noticed Brunelle glancing at her, she smiled and gestured for him to continue.

That meant she had a use for O'Brien on cross exam.

Double great.

"So, was blood revenge practiced by Northwest coastal tribes?" Brunelle asked.

"Yes." O'Brien turned to the jury. He was learning. "Yes, it was."

"And was it the same practice you described earlier?" Brunelle confirmed. "One member of a tribe is killed, so that tribe is allowed to kill a member of the other clan to settle the score?"

"Well, you see," O'Brien took off the glasses again, "it's not just that the offended tribe was allowed to commit the blood revenge killing. They were expected to do it. In fact, in a way, they had a duty to do it."

O'Brien stopped, perhaps getting used to being cut off by Brunelle. But this was where Brunelle wanted O'Brien to show off his knowledge, so he just nodded and said, "Go on."

"Yes, well, as I was saying." He turned again to the jury. Brunelle could see the academic was enjoying his captive audience. "The offended tribe—the one whose member was killed in the first place—had an obligation to carry out the blood revenge killing, even if perhaps they were reluctant to do so. You see, the practice was not terribly unlike our modern criminal justice system. The justifications usually put forward for criminalization and incarceration are deterrence and retaliation. It was no different with blood revenge. Knowing that one of your own will be killed if you kill one of theirs serves to keep you from killing one of theirs in the first place. It helps discourage both intentional killings and recklessness that might lead to a death. But that deterrence breaks down if there is doubt as to whether the blood revenge killing will actually be carried out."

Brunelle nodded along. *Stage two complete. Time for stage three.*

"Were there ever instances when something less than a killing could be accepted as payment for the first killing?"

O'Brien rubbed his hands together. "Oh, yes. As you can imagine, the death of anyone is tragic, but practically speaking, it can also be quite disruptive to the economic wellbeing of a tribe that needed every member to help it make it through another hunting season or harvest. That was part of the reason for the deterrence. Few tribes could afford to lose very many members that way. So sometimes the offended clan would accept a monetary payment rather than blood revenge: foodstuffs, skins, et cetera. This paid—at least in part—for the economic impact of the loss of the tribal member, and the other clan was still deterred by the payment. They were willing to pay it because it might pale in comparison to the impact of losing a member of their own tribe."

Final stage.

"So, to summarize," Brunelle said, "if a member of one tribe was killed, then and only then was it okay to kill a member of the killer's tribe?"

"Er, yes." O'Brien frowned. "That's a bit simplistic, but basically it."

Brunelle managed a smile at the response.

"And the the blood revenge killing was both expected and accepted by both tribes?"

"More or less," O'Brien answered. "There was an expectation that it would be carried out."

"But sometimes, the offended tribe could allow the offending clan to pay the debt with something other than another killing."

"Correct." O'Brien nodded. "If the offended tribe so chose."

One last point, then sit down without ever suggesting that child molestation couldn't justify a murder. That was the obvious argument. But he'd save that for closing, lest O'Brien soft sell it like he did at the café.

"Professor, I believe you were about to say that this practice of blood revenge and blood feuds became such a problem that some tribes actually confederated together in order to eliminate the us versus them upon which the practice was based."

"Yes, that's true."

"So it sounds like, if some tribes would rather have received payment than revenge, and other tribes abandoned the practice altogether, maybe it wasn't such a great thing after all?"

O'Brien shook his head. "I wouldn't say that. It served a purpose."

"But that purpose has passed, hasn't it, professor?"

O'Brien considered for a moment. "Yes, I would say that it has."

"Thank you." Brunelle stepped toward his counsel table. "No further questions."

He sat down, happy with how his direct had gone. He knew Talon would score points on cross, but he'd scored what points he needed. O'Brien's words were like weapons thrown onto the coliseum sand for the gladiators to pick up and use in closing argument. He didn't need O'Brien to say specifically that Traver needed to consent to the blood revenge, he'd just argue that in closing based on what O'Brien did say.

"Cross examination, Ms. Winter?" the judge asked.

Talon stood up and flashed her predatory smile. "Absolutely, Your Honor. But I'll be brief."

Brunelle suppressed a wince. 'Brief' meant 'focused.' And focused cross was always the most effective.

"Hello, Professor O'Brien," Talon sidled up to the witness stand. All smiles. Like a big cat, warm and fuzzy—claws hidden from her prey. "You seem to be quite the expert on these matters."

O'Brien smiled too. "Well, I do have a doctorate."

Just in case the jury had forgotten to hate him. Brunelle sighed to himself.

"Yes," Talon agreed. "I was going to ask you about that. This is all an academic exercise for you, isn't it?"

Oh, fuck. O'Brien didn't know what was about to hit him, but Brunelle did.

"I'm not quite sure I follow you," O'Brien replied.

"Well, let's approach it a different way," Talon said. "Based on your research, do you feel comfortable saying that blood revenge was limited to a killing in retaliation for a killing, not something less?"

O'Brien removed his glasses again and pointed them at Talon. "You know, Mr. Brunelle and I discussed that very matter the first time we met."

"Oh, did you now?" Talon turned and smiled at Brunelle. He nodded in return but otherwise maintained his poker face. "And tell me, what did the two of you discuss?"

"Well, it was very interesting." Again the hand-rubbing. "We discussed whether something like what happened here—the sexual assault of a child—could rise to the level of authorizing a blood revenge killing."

"How interesting," Talon said. "What did you decide?"

O'Brien frowned and turned back to the jury. "It's actually a very complicated question," he said. "You see, sexual mores and the roles of women and children were quite different from what we might expect today—"

"Excuse me, professor." Talon's voice cut through the room. "Are you saying my ancestors condoned the molestation and rape of children?"

Brunelle was impressed. Obviously a well-rehearsed trap. And O'Brien walked right into it.

The professor's face flushed. "Uh, well... I don't mean that exactly. It's just that... Um... Things were different."

"And you know that from reading books?"

"Well, yes. That and—"

"And what, professor?" Talon cut in. "No, wait. Let me ask you a different question."

"Uh, okay," O'Brien said meekly. The blood was draining from his face, leaving blotches at his ears and neck.

"You're here to tell this jury what their culture is, correct?"

O'Brien's eyebrows knitted together. "I don't think that's a fair characterization of—"

"You don't have a drop of Indian blood, do you, Professor O'Brien?"

He grimaced. "Er, no. As you said, my last name is O'Brien. I'm mostly Irish and German, with some other stuff thrown in."

"Other stuff, but no Native American, right?" Talon confirmed.

"Well," O'Brien started.

Don't, thought Brunelle. *Just don't.* But it was too late.

"There's a family legend," O'Brien offered, "that we've got Blackfoot somewhere back on my mom's side, but nothing I can prove."

"I see." Talon nodded. "Just the White Man wishing he had a bit of the exotic and noble savage coursing through his veins, huh?"

O'Brien shrugged. "Perhaps so."

Talon nodded again and pressed her hands together. Her nails were perfect, a French manicure but with red tips instead of white. Bloodied claws.

"So let me ask you this." She moved in for the kill. "Since you're here to tell us how we should feel about ourselves, do you know what it feels like to be the only dark person in the room?"

O'Brien started to answer, not realizing his answer wasn't the point.

"Do you know what it feels like when someone stares at you, trying to figure out, not *who* you are, but *what* you are? How do *you* feel, sir, when someone asks if you're Asian? Or Filipino? Or Hispanic? And it doesn't even occur to them that you're Native?"

"Yes, well..." O'Brien tried, but to no avail.

"How do *you* feel, Professor William O'Brien, Ph.D., on Thanksgiving, when this country pretends to celebrate the one time they didn't slaughter your ancestors, and you turn on the TV only to see the Cowboys play against the God damned '*Redskins*'?! How does *that* make you feel, professor?"

O'Brien sat silently for several seconds, staring at the very beautiful and very angry woman in front of him. "I don't know how that feels."

"Damn right you don't." Talon spun on her heel and strode back to counsel table. "No further questions."

CHAPTER 40

"How goes trial?" Chen asked over the phone.

"Oh, swimmingly," Brunelle answered as he stood on his hotel room balcony watching the city lights twinkle off the water. "My Indian expert is a racist. Did you know that?"

"So are you," Chen jabbed. "They're Native Americans, not Indians."

"Don't you start too," Brunelle chided as he took a bite of last night's pizza. "Now, you got any news for me?"

"Nothing yet," Chen admitted. "I double checked the property sheets and interviewed every property room officer. No one looked at the property or even requested it after you and I did our viewing."

"So what happened? Inside job?" Brunelle suggested. "Someone in the property room playing a joke?"

"Not a very funny joke," Chen observed. "I don't think that's it."

"So what do you think it is?" Brunelle could hear that 'I've got an idea' tone in Chen's voice.

"I'll tell you after I prove it," Chen replied.

"What if you don't?"

"Then I don't tell you," Chen explained. "You don't get a rep as a premier detective by telling everyone all your half-baked theories that don't pan out."

"Larry?"

"Yeah?"

"I hate to tell you this, but that's not your rep."

"You liar," Chen laughed. "You didn't hate to tell me that."

Brunelle took another bite of pizza and shook his head. "How about our other issue?"

"Hernandez?"

"Yeah."

"Still on life support," Chen reported. "But still alive too."

Well, that's all I can ask for, I guess."

"That, and an expert who's not racist," Chen joked. "Like you are."

Brunelle almost managed a laugh. "Thanks, pal. I'm going to hang up now."

There was a pause, then Chen said, "Call her."

"Who? The defense attorney? Man, did you notice how hot she w—"

"No, dumb ass. Not the defense attorney."

"Oh."

"Call her. Keep calling her."

Brunelle nodded, but was glad Chen couldn't see it. "Goodbye, Larry."

CHAPTER 41

The remainder of Brunelle's case-in-chief was decidedly less interesting, but it had to be done. Everyone knew Quilcene was the killer, but Brunelle actually had to put on the evidence to prove it. So there was a parade of technical witnesses. Forensics officers who collected evidence, like the knife and the swabs of blood from Quilcene's hands. Fingerprint analysts who linked Quilcene to the knife. The crime lab scientist who confirmed the blood on Quilcene's hands was Traver's. Plus a few patrol officers who filled in the gaps of the investigation. He never did manage to find an eyewitness to the murder. The only ones who claimed to have seen it were either too drunk to remember, or long gone.

True to form, Talon knew these witnesses were necessary for Brunelle, but not necessary to cross. It was Traver's blood on her client's hands. What was she going to ask? So while it was a tad boring, with minimal cross, it went quickly. Brunelle rested his case on Thursday confident he had proved Quilcene killed Traver, but less sure the jury would label it murder.

He was glad to be done. It was always a relief to rest the case. Plus, he was—out of professional respect and curiosity—

looking forward to seeing what Talon put on. As it turned out, he had to wait one more day.

"We will stop early today," Judge LeClair announced when Brunelle rested shortly after lunch. "And begin first thing in the morning with Ms. Winter's opening statement to the jury. Court is adjourned."

As the judge and jurors and spectators and media began to file out of the courtroom, Talon came over to where Brunelle was collecting his things.

"Ready to get your ass kicked?" she teased.

Brunelle feigned a pained expression and rubbed his backside. "I thought you did pretty well just cross examining my witnesses. My ass is pretty sore already."

Talon looked at his ass and smiled—a bit enigmatically, he thought. "That's just the beginning, Dave. I promise."

"You still going with that loser defense of justifiable homicide?" he asked as he closed his briefcase. The question was part conversation, part preparation. He certainly wouldn't mind knowing what she was going to say in advance of her saying it.

Talon grinned, her lips red and full. "You know that's never really been the defense, Dave."

Brunelle cocked his head. "I'm pretty sure you endorsed that defense way back at our first meeting with the judge. Before the arraignment even."

"Don't play dumb, Dave," she replied, crossing her arms. It still made his heart race every time she said his name. "We both know the real defense. The real reason I'll win this case is because he deserved it. Hell, your detective admitted as much. The jury will want to acquit my guy. They just need an excuse. Blood revenge is that excuse."

Brunelle smiled, but didn't say anything. The smile had two

sources. First, Talon really was one hell of a lawyer. She knew the secret to successful trial work was giving the jury an excuse to do what they want to do anyway. The second reason was that he had buried a bomb under her defense—one he wasn't going to detonate until closing arguments, when he could also remind the jury that it didn't matter a damn what they wanted to do, they had a duty to follow the law.

Talon saw the smile. "I know you don't think much of the defense. It grabs the attention, but it's too complicated, what with all that trying to figure out what the tribal law on blood revenge was at the time the treaty was ratified and how to apply it now and blah, blah, blah."

Damn. She's even pretty when she says, 'Blah, blah, blah.'

"Well," Brunelle forced out the thought, "I have confidence in your ability to explain it to the jury."

Talon winked. She actually winked. His heart swelled and he hoped he wasn't starting to blush. "Thank you, kind sir. So do I. But, just in case a few of them don't get it, I'll be giving them at least one more reason to acquit."

Brunelle frowned. He could guess what she was going to do. "You have to give me advance notice of a self defense claim, you know. Not spring it on me after I rest."

Talon laughed. Damn, he liked that laugh. "It's not a full self defense claim, Dave. I'm not going to ask the judge to explain it or instruct on it. Hell, that's even more confusing than justifiable homicide. But I imagine when my poor little client testifies—"

"Your poor little murderous gang-banger," Brunelle corrected.

"When my poor little client," Talon insisted, "testifies, he might just mention how much bigger and meaner and drunker Traver was that night. How he'd heard all the terrible things Traver had done. How he just didn't know what else Traver was capable of."

"He molested pre-schoolers behind closed doors," Brunelle pointed out. "He was a coward. He wouldn't take on a nineteen-year-old gang thug."

"Exactly," Talon agreed. "Unless he was armed. Which is why my poor, innocent client thought he was reaching for a weapon." She narrowed her eyes as her lips curled into that tiger's smile. "It was *so* dark that night."

"Pioneer Square is practically flood-lit on a Saturday night," Brunelle pointed out.

"So dark," Talon repeated, raising her hands to her mouth in faux-terror, "and so big and so dangerous. And oh! Is he reaching for a weapon? Whatever shall I do?"

Brunelle crossed his arms. "Are you going to testify for him too?"

Talon laughed again. That sexy damn laugh. "Oh, no. He's going to do way better than that."

"Great."

"I think," Talon purred, "your ass may never stop hurting."

"So, you starting with him?" Brunelle wanted to know what to prep for the morning.

"Nope. Better. Way better."

"Who?"

"Caitlyn's mommy. I need to remind the jury why they want to acquit."

CHAPTER 42

"My client, Johnny Quilcene, killed George Traver."

Talon began her opening statement quietly. Her hands were clasped in front of her conservative, dark gray suit and cream-colored blouse.

"But he didn't *murder* him."

"Objection," Brunelle jumped on it. "Argumentative."

He knew he was right and the objection should be sustained. He also figured it wouldn't be. Might as well test the waters at the beginning.

"Overruled," LeClair said, barely looking at him. "You may continue Ms. Winter. And try not to interrupt any further, Mr. Brunelle."

Brunelle nodded. If that wasn't going to be sustained as argumentative, nothing was. No point in objecting any more. At least, he could relax and enjoy the show.

"The evidence," Talon continued, "which Mr. Brunelle put on about the facts of this case is true. But it was incomplete. My client did stab George Traver. He did leave the knife behind. Those were his fingerprints on the knife. That was Mr. Traver's blood on his hands. And he did say that Mr. Traver deserved it."

She paused.

"And he did."

"Obj—" Brunelle started. Then, looking up at LeClair. "Never mind. Sorry. Automatic reaction."

Talon glared at Brunelle for a split second, then turned her confident half-smile back to the jury. "He did deserve it. Not in an abstract, 'people get what they deserved instant karma kind of way of deserving something. No. He deserved it under the law. The killing was justified."

She waited a moment, glancing at Brunelle to see if he might object again. The judge looked at him too. He peered up from his notepad long enough to shake his head slightly. He was done objecting. It wouldn't do any good, and the jury would get sick of him continually interrupting. Besides, his expert had testified and, blistering cross exam notwithstanding, the jury would view everything Talon said through the prism of his testimony.

Talon returned to her presentation. "This case is here in this court with you good people as jurors because of a treaty signed decades ago between our sovereign nation—"

'Our,' Brunelle noticed. *Nice touch.*

"—and the government of the United States. And because of that, you will get to apply our tribal law as it existed then. Including the law of blood revenge.

"Now, you've already heard from the prosecution. Mr. Brunelle drives down from Seattle to tell you what your culture is. To help him, he brings an Irish-German professor from Iowa to tell you what your culture is. But you know what, ladies and gentleman? Don't let these outsiders tell you what your culture is. You know it already. You know what's right and you know what's wrong. What's wrong is what happened to Caitlyn. And what's right is what happened to George Traver."

Brunelle scanned the faces of the jurors to see their reaction to that assertion. He hoped someone would cross their arms, or look away, or frown. But nothing. All faces remained fixed on Talon. So he looked back at her too.

"You're going to hear from several witnesses. You'll hear from Stacy Quilcene, Caitlyn's mother. She'll explain exactly how Traver's crime against Caitlyn impacted her family. Then you'll hear from a real expert on our culture, Doctor Joseph Red Deer. He not only holds the academic credentials, but is Native himself.

"And finally you'll hear from my client, Johnny Quilcene. He will testify about what his sister Stacy told him. And worse: what his niece Caitlyn told him. He'll tell you he reported the incident to the police but they did nothing."

Brunelle looked up from his note-taking. That was the first he'd heard about Quilcene ever reporting the molestation.

"Johnny will tell you that he went up to Seattle to confront George Traver. He'll tell you Traver admitted he molested Caitlyn. He refuse to apologize. In fact, he laughed about it."

Brunelle doubted that was true, but such was the dilemma of having no witnesses to the argument. Quilcene could say whatever the hell he wanted, with no worry he would be contradicted.

"And so," Talon continued, "Johnny chose the option bequeathed to him by his—by our ancestors. He avenged what happened to his sweet, innocent, defiled niece."

Talon paused. All eyes, even Brunelle's, were on her.

"Ladies and gentlemen, at the end of this trial I will stand up again and ask you to affirm our culture, and our traditions, and our law. I will ask you stand up against what's wrong and stand up for what's right. I will ask you to help avenge the murder, not of

George Traver, but of Caitlyn Quilcene's innocence.

"I will ask you to render the only just verdict in this case: not guilty. Thank you."

Not bad, Brunelle thought. *But not great either*. He still had a chance.

Time to see what Caitlyn's mom had left to say.

CHAPTER 43

There was no good way to cross examine the mother of a child molestation victim.

Brunelle knew Talon called her first because her whole case was built on painting him and O'Brien and Chen and Kat and everyone else as outsiders. As people who just didn't understand. Or, more importantly, didn't care.

So, while there was a definite value to the defense in the information Talon would elicit in during her direct examination, the real prize for Talon would lay in Brunelle's vigorous and heartless cross examination of the broken-hearted mother of the real victim in the case.

"Please remind the jury," Talon started as Stacy sat in the witness chair, "who you are and how you're related to the case."

"Stacy Quilcene," she answered, her demeanor at once more relaxed and more sympathetic than when Brunelle had called her. "My brother is the defendant. My daughter was molested by George Traver."

"I'm sorry for that," Talon said.

Stacy looked down. "Thank you."

Brunelle managed not to roll his eyes. It was a nice touch—likely rehearsed. He thought it was maybe a bit too much. But he would have done the same thing.

"When did you tell your brother," Talon moved on, "about what happened to Caitlyn?"

"Right after she told me," Stacy answered, starting to tear up already. "I— I was just so shocked. I had to tell someone, so I called Johnny. He's the one we all call if we need something. He takes care of us."

With money his gang makes selling drugs and chopping cars, Brunelle thought. He jotted a note about that. Just because he wasn't going to defend Traver's character didn't mean he couldn't attack Quilcene's.

"How did Johnny react when you told him?"

Stacy shook her head. "He was great. He reacted just right, you know? The first thing he did was check on Caitlyn. He told her he loved her and it wasn't her fault."

"Good for him," Talon said.

Wow. Brunelle decided not to object to Talon's commentary. He wanted to, but he knew the jury would think he was being mean.

"Did Johnny mention anything about confronting Traver, or settling the score, or anything like that?"

"Not at first, no. His first concern was Caitlyn. Then me. I was a wreck. I couldn't stop crying. I'd failed my baby. I let this happen. I was supposed to protect her and I didn't."

Then she totally lost it. Deep, loud sobs filled the courtroom as Stacy's pain and guilt spilled out for all to see.

"Do you need a moment?" Talon asked.

But Stacy couldn't even respond. Brunelle expected the judge to call a recess for her to compose herself, but he didn't. They just sat there, listening to the wails of a broken mother until she could calm down enough to speak again.

Talon handed her some tissue and waited patiently until Stacy finally stopped crying—audibly, at least—and wiped her nose, and squeaked, "I'm sorry, I think I can go on."

"Don't be sorry," Talon replied. "Don't ever be sorry. It wasn't your fault. It was Traver's fault."

"Objection, Your Honor," Brunelle finally felt compelled to say. "Counsel keeps commenting on the testimony, rather than asking questions."

LeClair frowned. "I'm going to allow some leeway, given the nature of the testimony. But do try to limit your comments, Ms. Winter."

"Yes, Your Honor," Talon replied. "I am trying."

Brunelle sat down again, not sure whether that exchange had helped or hurt him. *Poor Talon. She just can't help but care. Puke.*

"So Johnny took care of Caitlyn and he took care of you," Talon reminded the jury. "Did he call anyone?"

"Y-yes," Stacy sniffled. "He called the cops."

"Did they come out and take a report?"

"Yeah, like two days later," Stacy practically spat. "Some detective who told us that they'd never be able to prove it because Caitlyn was too young to testify. He was real jerk. Some old guy with a mustache a bunch of stripes down his sleeve. He said we should have taken her to the hospital right away for a rape exam, but it was too late now. But if they'd told us that when Johnny called, instead of waiting two days, we would have done that."

"So the police weren't very helpful then?"

"Hell no."

"Was it the tribal police?"

"Yeah," Stacy answered. "'Cause it happened on the

reservation."

"Did they refer it to the Tacoma Police or the Pierce County Sheriff's Department?"

"They didn't refer it to anyone." Stacy shook her head, her teeth clenched. "Johnny had to call again a week later. They told him Traver had stopped registering, they didn't know where he was, and there was nothing more they could do."

"And is that when Johnny decided to go find Traver?"

"I guess so." Stacy nodded. "He told me he was going to find the man who did that to Caitlyn and make things right."

"Did he explain what he meant by 'make things right'?"

"Nope," Stacy said. "And I didn't ask."

Talon nodded, as if she hadn't already heard this story a half-dozen times. "Did he show you anything before he left?"

Stacy sniffled again and offered a quiet, "Yes." She knew what the next question was going to be.

Talon nodded to the bailiff and he extracted the cardboard box from its secure location under his desk. Talon took it and opened it for Stacy to see inside. It was the knife, already admitted into evidence during Brunelle's case-in-chief.

"Is this what he showed you?"

"Yes," Stacy answered. "That's my grandpa's knife. *Our* grandpa's knife. He carved the handle himself."

"So it holds special significance for your family?"

"Oh yes." Stacy turned to the jury to explain. "When grandpa died, we kept it in a special box. Our family doesn't have much, but that knife was special."

Talon nodded. She shifted gears, ever so slightly. "Do you know whether Johnny usually carried a weapon?"

"Oh no," Stacy was quick to reply.

Of course not, Brunelle thought sarcastically. *What self-*

respecting gang member would ever carry a weapon?

"I mean," Stacy continued, "he knows some people who do carry—"

Fellow NGBs.

"—but not Johnny."

"Okay," Talon summarized. "So after you told him what Traver did to Caitlyn, and after the police said they weren't going to do anything, that's when Johnny—who doesn't normally carry a weapon—took your grandfather's ceremonial knife and said he was going to confront Traver and make things right?"

"Yes."

"No further questions."

Talon sat down and Judge LeClair glared down at Brunelle. "Any cross examination?" he practically challenged.

Brunelle stood up.

Your brother is a member of the Native Gangster Bloods street gang, isn't that correct?

He is more than accustomed to violence, right?

He didn't know anything about some ancient rite of blood revenge, did he?

He was just angry and wanted to hurt the man who'd hurt his niece, right?

"No questions, Your Honor. Thank you."

He sat down again.

There was no good way to cross examine the mother of a child molestation victim.

CHAPTER 44

"Joseph Red Deer," Talon's expert smiled to the jury. He was central casting for Native American academic. Tall, not skinny but not fat, deep skin tone, and black hair pulled back into a pony tail and just beginning to gray at the temples.

"Where do you work, Mr. Red Deer?" Talon asked from her spot in the attorney well.

"I am the assistant director of the Northwest Native American Museum in Kelso, Washington."

"And in that capacity, are you familiar with the customs and traditions of the Northwest coastal tribes?"

"In that capacity and also personally," he nodded. "I am a member of the Quinault Nation."

"Are you familiar with a specific tradition known as blood revenge?"

"Yes," Red Deer told the jury with a subdued smile. "I am."

"Please tell us about it."

And so he did. It wasn't materially different from anything O'Brien had said. That was important. If it had been, then Brunelle would have needed to cross examine him hard on the differences.

But it was basically the same. And really, it should have been. O'Brien wasn't lying. He was just white. And more importantly, he was called by the prosecution, so the defense felt the need to call a competing expert. Except that when the defense expert agreed with the prosecution expert, there wasn't much competition. Still, Brunelle listened patiently. He knew exactly where their opinions would diverge. Everyone agreed blood revenge existed. They just disagreed about whether it still applied. Or should.

"So let me ask you this," Talon sharpened her focus as she neared the end of her examination. "I'd like you to assume that the jurisdiction for this prosecution is based on the 1854 Treaty of Medicine Creek between the Puyallup Nation and the United States government. I'd like you to further assume that because of that, we are applying Puyallup tribal law at the time of the adoption of the treaty."

"All right," Red Deer answered slowly, as if Talon hadn't completely scripted this and likely even rehearsed it with him a few times.

"Was blood revenge the law at the time the treaty was adopted in 1854?"

Red Deer nodded thoughtfully. "Now, you see. Even that question fails to properly understand Native tradition."

A smile curled in the corner of Talon's mouth. "Please explain."

"Well, you asked me if that was the law, but the question assumes that Native cultures passed and adopted laws like contemporaneous European cultures. In fact, tradition and custom played a far greater role in Native cultures than they did in European-based societies. European elites have a long tradition of passing laws in order to break traditions—to overpower cultural norms through legislative fiat and punishment. Indeed, Native cultures across the world have been the subject of such efforts by European colonists who outlaw Native cultures and languages in an effort to, in their words, civilize the Natives. You can see this from English efforts to eradicate Scottish and Irish culture to American atrocities like the Indian Schools and the Trail of Tears.

"But in Native societies, traditions weren't just important, they were sacred. To say something was tradition was tantamount to saying it was the law. And blood revenge was absolutely an accepted Native tradition."

Talon's nodded. "Thank you, sir. No further questions."

LeClair looked down. "Any cross examination, Mr. Brunelle?"

"Yes, Your Honor," he answered as he stood up. "Briefly."

One thing Brunelle knew was to never argue with an expert while he was still on the stand. Argue with him in closing argument when he can't respond.

O'Brien had said the offending tribe understood that blood revenge would be coming and they were supposed to accept it. Red Deer just said blood revenge was an accepted tradition. So Brunelle could tell the jury, in closing, that Red Deer had agreed with O'Brien that blood revenge was only allowed if the offending tribe,—or in this case George Traver—knew blood revenge would be coming and he was supposed to accept it. There was no way Talon could credibly argue that Traver knew he would be killed for molesting Caitlyn, let alone that he would accept it, so therefore Red Deer supported the prosecution's theory and the defendant is guilty.

Great closing. Terrible cross. Ask Red Deer to agree with that and he'd turn to the jury and explain exactly why Brunelle was a full of shit.

So instead, Brunelle asked him, "Blood revenge wasn't

limited to Native American tribes, was it?"

Red Deer frowned. "Well, my expertise is mainly with Native cultures."

"Okay." Brunelle could see he'd need to guide him a little bit. Maybe just as well. Show the jury he'd thought about the idea himself. "You've heard of 'an eye for an eye, a tooth for a tooth,' right?"

Red Deer grinned. "Of course."

"And that was similar to blood revenge, correct?"

"I suppose," Red Deer agreed after a moment. "Although it seems to address transgressions short of killing."

My point exactly, Brunelle thought. Although he wondered how he could argue that the proper revenge against Traver would have been to sexually assault him, rather than kill him.

"And are you familiar with the Latin phrase 'lex talionis'?" Brunelle asked, then translated, "The law of the talion."

"I believe," Red Deer replied, "it was a similar concept."

"Right," Brunelle said. "If you damage someone, you will be damaged in the same way."

"Okay," Red Deer replied.

"And are you familiar with Professor Miller's work on Icelandic sagas and blood feuds?"

Red Deer offered a half smirk. "Uh, no. I'm afraid I'm not."

Well, good. Neither am I.

Brunelle took a few steps away from the witness stand then turned around again. The purpose was to get everyone to look at him, not Red Deer. "But will you agree with me that many European-based societies practiced some sort of retributive justice similar to the concepts underpinning blood revenge?"

Red Deer thought for a moment, then nodded. "I think that's a true statement."

"But 'lex talionis' isn't the law in Italy any more, is it?"

Red Deer smiled. He got it. "No, I don't believe so."

"And they aren't stabbing people's eyes out in courts in Israel, are they?"

"No." The smile tightened a bit. "I don't believe they are."

"And last time I checked, there are no Viking blood feuds raging in Iceland, right?"

"Last I checked," Red Deer agreed.

"Even the Hatfields and the McCoys have stopped fighting, isn't that right?"

"I haven't heard much about that feud recently," Red Deer replied.

"So..." Brunelle stepped back to the witness stand. "Are you telling me that the Puyallup Nation is alone among civilized people in still condoning vigilante revenge killings?"

The smile melted away, but Red Deer didn't say anything.

Brunelle waited for the reply. He didn't mind. What really mattered was his question. And every second Red Deer delayed just showed how much he didn't want to admit the answer.

"I'm saying blood revenge was an important tradition for many Native people, including the Puyallup."

"So, the Puyallup Indian Reservation is the one place in the civilized world where it's acceptable—required even—for neighbor to murder neighbor?"

"Of course not," Red Deer started. "That's not—"

Brunelle interrupted. "Of course not, you said?"

"Yes. Of course not."

Brunelle smiled. "I think you're absolutely right. Thank you. No further questions."

Talon popped up before Brunelle even sat down. She didn't wait for the judge to inquire if she had more questions.

"But the difference is," she half-asked, half-stated, "that these other cultures decided to abandon that practice, whereas our laws and traditions were forcibly supplanted by so-called treaties that were rarely if ever honored, isn't that correct?"

It was a good question—despite being ridiculously objectionable as leading—but it didn't matter. Brunelle had made his point.

"Er, yes," Red Deer decided to agree with the lawyer who had called him. "I think there's a great deal of truth in what you just said."

"Thank you," Talon huffed. "No further questions."

"Any re-cross?" LeClair asked Brunelle.

"No, Your Honor," Brunelle stood to answer.

The judge turned to Red Deer. "You are excused. Then he turned to Talon. "Next witness, counsel."

Talon looked at the clock on the wall. It was only 2:40. There was plenty of time to call another witness. Hell, there was time for a few witnesses.

"May we excuse the jury for a moment?" she asked. "To discuss scheduling?"

The judge made that perturbed face judges make when they have to go to the trouble of sending the jury out just to have a two-minute conversation with the lawyers. Then he made that resigned face judges make when they know they have to do it anyway.

He turned to the jury. "Ladies and gentlemen, I'm going to excuse you to the jury room for a few minutes while the lawyers and I discuss scheduling. Thank you."

The bailiff escorted them out and once the door to the jury room closed, Judge LeClair looked down at Talon. "What do we need to discuss?"

"Your Honor, I apologize," Talon began. "But the next

witness we intend to call is the defendant himself."

Brunelle nodded. He'd expected as much based on the logical order of likely defense witnesses. He'd brought his materials for crossing Quilcene in case they got that far. Another reason to keep his earlier cross exams short.

"However," Talon went on. "As the court may have heard, a dear friend of my client was shot the other night and is in I.C.U. at Tacoma General. We got word over the lunch hour that he might not survive the day and my client would very much like a chance to say goodbye before it's too late."

Judge LeClair frowned at Talon, but didn't say anything.

"My client is in no condition to testify right now, Your Honor," Talon claimed. Then, obviously to remind the judge of how much he respected her professionalism, she added, "I thought I should mention this outside the presence of the jury as it might unfairly invoke sympathy for my client."

And give me the chance to mention their shared gang ties, Brunelle thought.

"I'm certain," Talon concluded, "that Mr. Brunelle wouldn't mind the extra time to prepare his cross examination of my client."

The judge looked at Brunelle.

"I don't need extra time to prepare," he said. He looked at Talon, who offered the slightest eyebrow raise. *Damn that pretty face.* "But I won't object to adjourning early today. I can sincerely say that I hope Mr. Quilcene's friend pulls through."

I just won't say why.

LeClair frowned, but he said, "All right then. We'll adjourn for the day. Bailiff, inform the jury they are excused for the day, but instruct them to be here at eight-forty-five tomorrow morning. We will start promptly at nine o'clock with the direct examination of the defendant by Ms. Winter. Court is adjourned."

The judge rose to leave and everyone in court honored the bailiff's call to "All rise!"

After he'd left, Talon stepped over to Brunelle. "Thank you."

Brunelle shrugged. "No problem. Like you said, more time to prepare. I'm going to kill him on the stand tomorrow."

Talon winked. "Not if he kills you first."

She laughed, but he didn't.

"It was a joke," she assured.

Brunelle looked at Quilcene, who could hear their every word.

He wasn't laughing either.

CHAPTER 45

Brunelle walked out to the parking lot. Even though it was the middle of the afternoon, the autumn sky was gray and dark, threatening one of those three-day Northwest rains that are never hard, but never let up.

He took his phone out and checked for messages. He had four new texts.

From Chen: *knife theft WAS inside job. sort of. call me.*

Chen again: *hernandez took turn for worse. still alive. barely. call me.*

And Chen again: *youre welcome. call her.*

Then Kat: *Larry said to call you. I said no. But I'll answer if you call me.*

Two clicks later and his phone was dialing Kat's number.

"Hello?" she answered.

God, he loved her voice.

"Hey," he said. "It's me."

"Yeah." A pause. "I can see that."

Brunelle paused too. "Uh, thanks for answering."

"Thank Larry," Kat replied. "He said you're not as big of a jerk as you seem sometimes."

"Uh, thanks," Brunelle said, "I think."

"So, I didn't expect you to call so early. You on a break or something?"

"We adjourned early for the day," Brunelle explained. "Gang-banger defendant wanted to go see his gang-banger best friend in the hospital before he dies from being shot because he's a gang-banger."

"Wow. Nice description. Very sensitive."

"Yeah, well, I hear I'm not as big of a jerk as I seem sometimes."

Kat laughed.

God, he loved her laugh.

"So," she asked, "you staying down there again tonight?"

"Yeah, might as well. The defendant takes the stand first thing tomorrow morning." He paused. "What are you doing tonight?"

"Well, I was thinking," she said. He thought he heard that purr she had sometimes, hiding just beneath the surface of her words. "I might take Lizzy's to her grandma's in Auburn to spend the night. There's no school tomorrow. It's a teacher planning day. And she hasn't seen my mom for a while."

"Hm. Good idea," Brunelle replied. "You know, Auburn's pretty close to Tacoma."

"Mm-hmm," she said. The purr was there, no doubt.

"And I found this great restaurant down here," Brunelle went on.

Kat laughed. "You liar. I know better. You've been eating take-out pizza from the casino."

Brunelle had to laugh too. "How do you know me so well already?"

"I'll pick you up at six," she said. "I actually do know some great restaurants down there."

Brunelle smiled. His biggest smile since he saw her at Donatello's. "Sounds great. I'll wait in front of the hotel. With bells on."

"Ooh," she purred again. "I would like to see that."

"And nothing else," he joked.

"Slow down, David. You don't want to get yourself arrested. Again."

"Ouch," he said. "See you at six, Kat."

"See you then, David."

~*~

Dinner was pleasant. Just plain nice. No arguing. No suspicions. Just small talk and some of the best Vietnamese food Brunelle had ever eaten. By the time they got back to his hotel room, it was after nine o'clock.

Brunelle pushed the door open for Kat to walk in first. She did and nodded approvingly as she made her way toward the balcony in the back.

"Nice digs, David. I'd compliment you on how tidy everything is, but I know that's the maid."

"Yeah, it's pretty nice," he said as he slipped the 'Do Not Disturb' sign on the door handle and closed the door. "And I'll have you know, I am quite tidy. The maid helps, but my place up in Seattle is just as clean and orderly."

Kat was admiring the view through the gauzy curtain. "I'll have to take your word for it. I've never been to your place."

Brunelle stepped in behind her. Too close. Just right. "We'll have to do something about that."

Kat turned around, right into Brunelle's arms. She raised her face, closed her eyes, and they kissed.

Brunelle put his hands on her waist and pulled her against him. She wrapped her arms around his neck and pushed her fingers through his hair. Their lips parted and he tasted her delicious tongue. She moaned lightly into his mouth, which only made him pull her tighter against him. He lowered his hands down her back and onto her pants, her curves filling his palms, her face filling his mind.

"Wait." She pushed him away suddenly, her breath racing. "Whoa. We need to slow down."

Brunelle's heart was racing too. "What? Why? Did I do something wrong?"

He'd barely done anything at all.

"No, no. That's not it," Kat assured. "It's just..."

She put a hand on his chest. "Slow," she said. "I need slow. Okay?"

Brunelle put his hands around her waist again. It took a moment for the blood to return to his brain, but his heart knew the right answer. "Okay. Of course."

He leaned down and gave her a quick kiss on the lips.

Kat exhaled deeply and laid her head on his chest. "Thanks. Sorry. It's just— It's been a while since Lizzy's dad and I divorced. Long enough, I know, but still..."

Brunelle stroked her hair. "No need to apologize. I'm not going to worry about where we're going, or how fast we get there. I'm just glad you're here right now."

Kat lifted her head and looked him the eye. "You damn lawyers. I never know if you mean what you say, or you just always try to say the right thing."

Brunelle smiled. "Maybe it's both."

Kat narrowed her eyes, then rested her head on his chest again. "Maybe," she sighed. "But I doubt it."

They stood there for a while, Kat's head on his chest, and Brunelle looking through the gauze at the city lights. He didn't say anything. He knew sometimes the right thing to say is nothing.

Finally Kat asked, without lifting her head, "Can we go for a walk?"

Brunelle thought for a moment about all the other things he'd rather be doing with her. "Of course. That sounds nice."

She looked up at him again. "You're a terrible liar."

He shrugged.

She pushed up on her toes and kissed him. "Thanks."

He stole one more kiss back. "Don't thank me for something I want to do. A friend told me that once." He pulled away and took her hand. "Let's go for a walk."

~*~

It was a nice night. The sky had cleared a bit, revealing a handful of stars and a thin moon glowing dimly behind broken clouds. Brunelle and Kat walked hand-in-hand along the industrial road that led under the freeway toward the casino and the more residential area behind it. It was cold enough that Kat leaned into him for warmth. He thought about letting go of her hand so he could put his arm around her, but there was something about holding her hand. It just felt right.

"So, is Lizzy doing a Nutcracker this year?" he asked.

Kat looked up at him. "Now why would you ask that?"

"Well, I remember she did ballet," he said. "And it's fall. Don't they start having practices soon?"

Kat laughed lightly. "They're not practices," she said. "They're rehearsals. And yes, they've already started."

She swung their hands back and forth.

"I'm just surprised," she went on. "You finally get me alone. I freak out, so we're on a romantic walk, holding hands. And you ask about my daughter."

Brunelle thought for a moment. "Well," he shrugged, "she's a pretty important part of your life."

"She sure is."

"Well then. I care too."

Kat stopped and pulled on his hand. "More trying to say the right thing?"

Brunelle shook his head. "More trying to say the truth."

Kat stared at him through narrowed eyes.

"What are you thinking?" he asked.

"I'm trying to decide whether to believe you."

"Maybe this will help." He leaned down and kissed her.

"That never helps," she giggled. "What am I going to do with you?"

Brunelle had some ideas, but just then his phone rang.

"Eh..." he hesitated. "It might be Chen. I was supposed to call him."

"Go ahead and answer it," Kat said and she pulled them back into their stroll.

Brunelle looked at the screen. "Yep, it's Chen." He pressed the screen. "Hey, Larry. What's up?"

"Mulholland just called me," Chen said rapidly. "Hernandez is dead. They unplugged him an hour ago."

Brunelle pulled them to a stop.

Kat looked up at him. "What is it?"

"There's more," Chen said. "It gets worse."

Just then a car came squealing around the corner and accelerated toward them. Brunelle could see the figure of someone leaning out of the driver's window, a gun in his hand.

"Gotta go, Larry. Call 911 for us."

"Us?" Brunelle heard Chen ask as he hung up the phone and pulled Kat into a sprint.

CHAPTER 46

"David!" Kat screamed. "What's going on?"

"Just come on!" Brunelle pulled her hand harder as the car accelerated toward them.

"I'm in heels, you jackass!" She tried to yank her hand away, but Brunelle held on tight.

"Then kick them off," he yelled. "And run as fast as you can."

"Why?"

The first shot rang out. Brunelle instinctively ducked although he knew it would have been too late by the time he heard the shot. It missed them. *Thank God.*

Kat finally understood the urgency of their situation. At least in part.

"Holy shit! Somebody's shooting at us." She kicked off her shoes and sprinted even ahead of Brunelle.

"It's that car," he said, catching up with her.

"Then let's go somewhere a car can't," she said and ran toward the locked gate of the tribal cemetery. "We can squeeze through the bars, but a car won't be able to get through."

They ran as fast as they could and disappeared through the

iron bars just as the car careened around the corner and screeched to a halt in front of the cemetery.

They ducked behind a large tree near the entrance, both out of breath.

"I think we're safe now," Kat panted.

Brunelle shook his head in the dark. "Not necessarily."

A light spilled out of the car as the driver opened his door and got out. He closed it again and disappeared into the gloom in front of the graveyard. After a moment, they could hear the gate clank as their pursuer pushed through the bars too.

"Come on," Brunelle whispered and grabbed Kat by the hand. They took off running up the hillside the cemetery occupied.

There were no lights so they had to navigate by the dim glow of the surrounding streetlights and what little moonlight filtered through the clouds.

"Ow!" Kat whispered as she banged into a grave marker. "Where are we going?"

"To the top of the hill."

"I can see that. Why?"

"To hide."

"Where?"

Good question. "I don't know."

They could hear the shooter's steps behind them, squelching in the wet grass. He swore once as he too presumably ran into a headstone. Brunelle and Kat reached the top of the hill and the back gate. They slipped through those iron bars too, but not without clanking, so any hope their pursuer might have stayed behind, searching the dark graveyard in vain, was lost.

"Where now?" Kat asked, scanning the street that ran behind the cemetery.

"There." Brunelle pointed to the house across the street. The one he'd seen for sale on his first day to the reservation. Maybe the back door was left unlocked for showings. They didn't have a lot of options.

He tugged her across the street and behind a row of privacy bushes most likely designed to block the cemetery from the view of the front yard. Finger to his lips to indicate silence, he led them to the back of the house. Sure enough, it was unlocked. As quietly as he could, Brunelle opened the door and they stepped inside. He closed it silently behind them and locked it, the deadbolt letting out a louder clank than he would have liked.

He took Kat's hand and led her deeper into the house. It was a two-story, so they took the stairs leading up from the front door, and quickly climbed to the top floor. They glided across the carpet and crouched in the back of one of the upstairs bedrooms.

"Please tell me you started carrying a gun like you said you would," Kat whispered.

Brunelle frowned. "It's in my hotel room. I can't wear it to court, so I always forget it."

"Hell of a time to forget it."

"We might not need it anyway. I think we may have lost him."

Then they heard the front door open.

Fuck. I didn't think they'd both be unlocked.

A moment later, footsteps began ascending the stairs.

CHAPTER 47

"Oh no," Kat whispered. "What are we going to do?"

Brunelle looked around. Dim moonlight barely lit the room. "Get in the closet. It's me he's after."

"Who is, David?"

"Just do as I say."

"But David..."

"Do it."

Kat stared at him. In the pale light, he could see the tears glinting in her eyes. She nodded, then stood up and slipped into the closet. Brunelle stood up too, just as Johnny Quilcene stepped into the doorway.

"Brunelle," he said flatly. He flipped on the light switch, temporarily blinding Brunelle. "Hernandez says hi."

Quilcene had a semi-auto leveled right at Brunelle's chest. Large caliber by the looks of it.

"I thought Hernandez was dead," Brunelle replied, trying to sound brave.

"He is," Quilcene seethed. "Thanks to you."

"Me? I didn't have anything to do with him getting shot."

"Sure," Quilcene scoffed. "And your fat prosecutor friend didn't stab Bobby either."

"Well, I'm still not sure about that," Brunelle replied. "I actually thought he did it too. But now I'm not so sure."

Brunelle thought for a moment. "Is that why you shot him when he stepped out of the police station? Because you thought he killed your cousin?"

"He did kill my cousin," Quilcene shouted. "And I didn't shoot him. Hernandez did." He flashed an evil smile. "I was just driving."

Brunelle nodded. "Well, an accomplice is guilty of the same crime as the principal."

Quilcene shook the gun. "Shut up, Brunelle. It's time to end this blood feud."

Brunelle threw his hands wide. "Are you fucking kidding me? Blood feud? You really bought into that bullshit?"

Quilcene seemed shaken by Brunelle's reaction. "Yeah, well, not at first. I didn't stick Traver because of no fucking blood feud bullshit. I stuck him because he diddled my niece. Fuck him. You don't fucking touch my niece. Nobody touches my family"

Brunelle nodded. "Yeah, I kinda knew that. So what's with the blood feud crap?"

Quilcene narrowed his eyes. "The blood feud started when your fucking partner stabbed my cousin. That was him taking blood revenge. Him and you were taking Traver's side."

"I never took Traver's side," Brunelle protested. "Between you and me, I'm glad he's gone. But you can't just go kill somebody."

"Tell that to your partner," Quilcene shot back. "At least Traver fucking deserved it. Bobby didn't do nothing to deserve a knife in his chest."

Brunelle thought for a moment. He guessed Quilcene's gang-banger cousin had probably done more than enough in his life to deserve a knife in the chest, but he decided against saying as much. "I'm sure he didn't. But I'm pretty sure Freddy didn't kill him either."

"How would you know that?"

"Because I accused him of it. I thought he'd done it and I told that. He denied it and stormed out of the police station. That's when you—or Hernandez, I guess—shot him."

Then Brunelle realized something. "How did you know Freddy was even there?"

Quilcene smiled again. "I got a tip."

"A tip?" Brunelle's brow furrowed. "From who?"

"Same guy who tipped me off that Hernandez was dead and you was walking down by the casino."

The furrow deepened. "Who, Johnny?"

Quilcene opened his mouth, but then didn't say anything. Instead, his face twisted into a pained grimace. A moment later, his eyes rolled up and his arm dropped down, the gun falling to the floor just before he did the same.

From out of the darkness behind him stepped Sixrivers, a simple hunting knife his hand, its blade glistening with blood.

Kat burst out of the closet. "Tommy! Oh, thank God it's you. Thank you. Thank you."

Sixrivers screwed up his face at her. "Kat? What are you doing here?"

She ran a hand through her hair. "Long story, Tommy. I'll tell you back at the precinct. Thank God Larry called you."

Sixrivers shook his head. "Chen didn't call me."

"Of course he didn't," Brunelle said, pulling Kat against him.

"What do you mean?" she asked. "Why not?"

"Because," Brunelle answered, his eyes fixed on Sixrivers, "Tommy is the one behind all this."

CHAPTER 48

"What?" Kat exclaimed. "Don't be ridiculous. Tommy just saved us."

"No," Brunelle corrected. "Tommy just silenced Quilcene before he could tell us that Tommy was the one who tipped him off about Freddy and then me."

Kat forced a laugh. "Come on, David. That's ridiculous." She turned to Sixrivers. "Tell him, Tommy."

Sixrivers' eyes were locked with Brunelle's "That's ridiculous," he said flatly.

"See?" Kat said, her voice cracking slightly. "It's ridiculous."

"But it's true," Brunelle said.

Kat looked at Sixrivers.

"Yep," Sixrivers said. "But it's true."

Then he looked at Kat. "Damn it, Kat. You weren't supposed to be here. This would have ended it."

"Ended what?" she asked.

"The blood feud," Brunelle answered. "I get that now. You

stabbed Quilcene's cousin. How'd you get the knife?"

"I didn't. Not for Bobby." Sixrivers waved the knife in his hand. "I used this one. Same size, roughly. But when I heard there'd been some confusion up there and you thought Quilcene's antique knife had gone missing, I got an idea. I went there and pretended to drop off property on a nonexistent case. When they told me there was no such case, I talked them into letting me look through the property room. I am a detective after all."

Brunelle recalled Chen's text. *Knife theft WAS an inside job. Sort of.*

"Then I planted it in your hotel room," Sixrivers said. "I figured getting arrested would finally scare you away. But I guess you're just too stupid."

"I guess so," Brunelle agreed. "'Cause I still don't understand why."

"Traver was a piece of shit," Sixrivers said. "He deserved to die, and you know it. When Johnny told me what Traver had done, it didn't take long to locate him up in Seattle, but Seattle P.D. wouldn't let me touch him. They said he was too valuable as an informant."

"Yeah, that was pretty shitty," Brunelle agreed. Kat remained silent, eyes wide.

"Yeah, real shitty," Sixrivers replied. "And my boss told me to stop wasting time on a case we couldn't prove. So I let Johnny know where Traver was and reminded him ballistics could be traced." Sixrivers shook his head. "But the dumb ass left the knife behind. Who leaves the fucking knife behind?"

"It got stuck in a rib," Kat explained reflexively.

Sixrivers nodded, then surrendered a sad smile. "Thanks. But it meant he got caught. And if he got caught, he'd talk. Eventually. I thought he would have thrown me under the bus right away, but I'll give the kid credit. He kept his mouth shut. Then that hotshot lawyer came up with the blood revenge defense and I got an idea."

"What idea, Tommy?" Kat asked. Brunelle had already figured it out.

"If Johnny walked," Sixrivers explained, "he'd have no reason to talk. So why not give his lawyer's bullshit theory some real support. And I got to take out a couple of gang members as a bonus."

"But what about Freddy?" Kat demanded.

"Yeah." Sixrivers shrugged. "That was too bad. Cost of doing business."

"Doing business?" Kat yelled. "You fucking killed him."

"No," he replied as he transferred the knife to his left hand and picked Quilcene's gun off the floor. "Hernandez killed him."

"And you killed Hernandez," Brunelle realized. "And now Quilcene. No more witnesses."

"Almost no more witnesses," Sixrivers corrected. He reached down and pulled Quilcene's gun out from under the body. "It's a shame I couldn't stop Quilcene from killing you two. But don't worry, I got here right after he shot you and we struggled. I ended up stabbing him in the back with his own knife."

He leveled Qulicene's gun at Brunelle's chest. "Goodbye, Brunelle. You should've stayed off the reservation."

A shot rang out.

"No!" screamed Kat.

Brunelle grabbed his chest. But there was no gunshot wound. No pain. He looked at Sixrivers. He was too close to have missed.

Sixrivers teetered, then crumpled forward onto Quilcene's body, blood staining the center of his back where he'd been shot.

Detective Mulholland raised his cell phone to his ear as he stepped into the light of the bedroom. "They're okay, Larry. We got here just in time. They're okay."

EPILOGUE

Brunelle walked into the coffee shop again. He didn't know the address; he couldn't even remember its name. He'd had to start at Talon's office and retrace his steps. The café held the same late afternoon atmosphere. Dishes clinking, espresso steaming, commuters in line to fuel up for their drives home. His date waited at the same table he'd sat at before. When he approached, she looked up.

"Hello, Mr. Brunelle," Kat said. "So nice to see you again."

He tipped his head to her and sat down. "The pleasure is all mine, Dr. Anderson."

"Maybe later," she joked. "For now, let's stick to coffee."

Brunelle laughed and looked around. "So why did you insist on this place? Were you down here for something else?"

"No," Kat smiled. "I'm claiming it. I don't want you to have a place you met another woman while standing me up. Now this is the place you and I had coffee after you met another woman here while standing me up."

Brunelle nodded. "I wondered why you wouldn't tell me over the phone. Very logical. As well as manipulative and controlling."

"Takes one to know one." She pulled her purse up off the floor and set it on the table. "Do you like my new purse?"

Brunelle appraised it. It was nice enough. "Sure."

"I got it for us," she said.

He raised an eyebrow. "Oh, yeah?"

"Yeah." She opened it and let him peer inside. He could see the butt of a gun sticking out of a built in holster.

"Wow."

"Apparently," Kat observed as she closed the purse again, "if we're going to date, I need to be armed. Glock G17. Nine millimeter. With polygonal rifling, so it's almost impossible to trace."

"Impossible to trace?" Brunelle leaned back slightly. "Is that a threat?"

"David, I'm a scientist. I don't threaten, I explain."

He smiled. "I thought lawyers explained things."

"No, lawyers lie. But I know that now, and I'm armed, so we're good."

Brunelle extended his hand across the table. "Yeah? We're good?"

Kat smiled and took his hand. "Yes. We're good."

END

THE DAVID BRUNELLE LEGAL THRILLERS
Presumption of Innocence
Tribal Court
By Reason of Insanity
A Prosecutor for the Defense
Substantial Risk
Corpus Delicti
Accomplice Liability
A Lack of Motive
Missing Witness
Diminished Capacity
Devil's Plea Bargain
Homicide in Berlin
Premeditated Intent
Alibi Defense
Defense of Others

THE TALON WINTER LEGAL THRILLERS
Winter's Law
Winter's Chance
Winter's Reason
Winter's Justice
Winter's Duty
Winter's Passion

ALSO BY STEPHEN PENNER
Scottish Rite
Blood Rite
Last Rite
Mars Station Alpha
The Godling Club

ABOUT THE AUTHOR

Stephen Penner is an attorney, author, and artist from Seattle.

In addition to writing the *David Brunelle Legal Thriller Series*, he is also the author of the *Talon Winter Legal Thrillers*, starring Tacoma criminal defense attorney Talon Winter; the *Maggie Devereaux Paranormal Mysteries*, recounting the exploits of an American graduate student in the magical Highlands of Scotland; and several stand-alone works.

For more information, please visit *www.stephenpenner.com*.

Made in the USA
Las Vegas, NV
21 January 2023

66007191R00138